Pancake
Hollow
Primer

A Hudson Valley Story

Pancake
Hollow
Primer

A Hudson Valley Story

by Laurence Carr

Codhill Press books
are published for David Appelbaum

First Edition
Printed in the United States of America
Copyright © 2011 by Laurence Carr

ISBN 1-930337-59-0

Text design by Alicia Fox
Cover design by Tony Davis
Photo by Gary Mathias

Some of the pieces have appeared in the following publications:
*Awosting Alchemy, A Gathering of the Tribes, Shawangunk Review,
Chronogram* and *In Search Of.*

Grateful thanks to James Sherwood as reader, proofer and supporter

Pancake
Hollow
Primer

A Hudson Valley Story

Other Codhill Press books by
Laurence Carr

The Wytheport Tales
(fiction)

Riverine: An Anthology of Hudson Valley Writers
(editor)

WaterWrites: A Hudson River Anthology
(co-editor)

Table of Contents

To Kay
who shares the journey

A
Brief
History

Palimpsest

House as time capsule, over-stuffed with the once revered
and now forgotten.
A world translucent, revealing its once was, now isn't.
Like stars in present who only live their past.
House as star, waving particles across the cosmos.
Handing down its history to those who take the time
to take the time.

The Old Trunk

Hidden away in the corner of a lonely room, the old trunk
sits and waits.
On top, a faded, peeling label, "Hamburg" perhaps?
Inside, old photo books of someone's family, austere
and slightly rigid.
Letters with postmarks from towns unknown.
With the latest news no longer new.
Two deeds of sale, and a partial list of all who passed
through and then passed on.
Yellowed scraps of paper, now brittle to the breath,
written by learned hands
in curls and arcs, a precision now lost.
From a dipping pen that skated across an icy sheet.
Ephemera so close to dust but once more revived.
A fading trail of ink leading down the path
to calming night.

Passing Through
a partial list

Nathaniel Selleck	1820
Millicent Selleck	1820
Augustus A. Thompson	1849
Elizabeth Ann Thompson	1849
Isaac Saxton	1855
Rachel Ellis	1871
Elmira Cooper	1871
Ira Cooper	1871
Andrew S. Halstead	1871
Sarah E. Halstead	1871
Caroline Halstead	1871
Stephen Halstead	1871
Silas Saxton	1872
James H. Barett	1872
Margaret S. Barett	1872
Edward L. Tompkins	1880
Marietta Tompkins	1880
Elizabeth B. Crook	1885
Catherine H. McNicholas	1885
Joseph Bernard	1897
Ben Pizzuti	1897
Domenico Costantino	1906
Mary Costantino	1914

Deed (The First)

May 1, 1820

Nathaniel and Millicent Selleck
To Isaac Saxton

Conveys:

Beginning at a stake and stones
at the northeast corner of the Town of Plattekill
running N. 55 d. 36 m.W. along the Paltz line
13 chains 90 links to a stake and stones
thence
S. 8 d. 15 m. W. 4 chains 83 links
to a chestnut tree the north side of the road
and east of the Brook;
thence
across the road S. 34 d. 30m. East
3 chains 48 links to a stake in a ditch
thence
south 1 d. West 10 chains 72 links
to a stone wall of William St. Johns land,
thence
S. 73 d. 30 m. East along the wall
to a flat rock on the side of the road
with a stone upon it
thence
North 22 d. 14 m. East 12 chains 62 links
to a place of beginning.

Deed (The Second)

May 15, 1823

Conveys:

All that piece of land
lying in the town of Plattekill
aforesaid being part of Durham Patent
and begins at the chestnut tree
marked in the southeast corner of the land
now owned by Charles Young
and runs
thence
South 73 d. East 5 chains 25 links
to a stake and heap of stones
thence
South 18 degrees West
18 chains and 20 links
to a stake and heap of stones
being Abraham Wooley's
northwest corner bounds
thence
North 73 degrees West
5 chains 25 links
to a heap of stones
being Haydock Carpenter's
northwest corner of a wood lot
thence
North 18 degrees East
18 chains 20 links
to the place of beginning.

Funtz's Last Walk
(1899–2001)

Funtz, now in his 101st year, a life that spanned three centuries, wanders into the winter woods looking for that thing he'd misplaced last spring. He knows it's there if he'd only look hard enough. And with that same kind of deliberate thought, the kind that had been with him all these years, he'd also remember what it was he was looking for.

It was something he'd set down in an idle moment, then forgotten. Last spring probably. And now, here he is, out into the folds of chilly air, snow ankle deep to search for it. The wind sings a song from the old days before the apple trees went wild. Branches rub themselves together to keep warm, then drum against the hollow trunks. A forest of drums, and song, and silent snow. Freshly fallen over the night. He walks foot by footfall deeper into the woods. His woods. Down pathways he laid—when?

How long have I been in the hollow? Eighty some odd years—odd and even. The best of all worlds.

He'd slept little these last days. So little need for it now. And sometimes troubled sleep. Tight knit brows with furrows deep enough to plant potatoes.

Potatoes.

He remembers walking behind Grandfather in that field so long away, so far ago. Dropping quartered potatoes, staring back at him. Into earthy furrowed brows. That smell of rot and shit, sweet comfort then and still. Earth to earth, turning into dark roast crumble pie. With its uprising sprouts, its eyes seeking light. And in nearby rows, heads of cabbage with thoughts only of themselves.

Funtz got his name from the old Jewish tailor when he was not one day out of the womb. And only five years later he boarded the ship, a majestic mountain when you're five, bound for America. Wherever that was. He remembers the ship. Now just a rusting bathtub in a fading memory. Steerage back to back with Mama and Johan and the rest of the continent. All faded now. Like the ground he walks. White with quiet snow. Only the fox's dotted eyes glow black.

He remembers how he cried all the way over. Only pausing to catch his breath when he sat on the lap of Captain Consolation. Pulling at his white beard to gape his mouth full of jovial laughter. Crossing the water. Then crossing themselves with every bell. His bellwether, weather beaten. His life's journey from boy to man.

He remembers big brother Johan's voice, now long gone. He remembers it as if it was…

Look Funtz, Lady Liberty. Holding up a flaming sword, she broke it off in battle. And her book.

We knew those copper pages held the list of those she's letting in, and we hoped our names were written down there somewhere. But all we got was her cold stare. Mama looked up at her face and vomited her gruel. Our passage ended. Now to walk the plank in search of pirate gold. New World plunder. We'd heard the stories.

Soles touch land. Every breath is new air—never been breathed before. Mama and Johan and little Funtz. A Valkyrie and her two princes. Hiding her cough. Lucky day that one—a German checks our papers, eyes and ears and throats. We escape with our names not even misspelled, and the route to

Germantown. A few old coins wrapped in a hankie around my neck, telling them it's garlic. Later cheated into pennies by those who'd been there longer.

I should have shin-kicked the bastard with his oily grin. Then on to bread and broth and that smelly blanket. Camphor? Staying at a cousin's, or that's what we called him. The fifth floor walkup, Slovaks across the hall, Poles next door. We talk in sign language. The next day the work begins, like I'd never left. Carrying apple boxes that come downriver. Where the Italians live. Five cents a day, workman's wages. A man now, I pay for the soup greens.

He learns English three words a day. At the end of a week, a sentence. At the end of a month, a story. A year goes by—he speaks "Dutch English." Mama turns American. In her bed, she finds peace reciting state capitals: Albany, Annapolis, Augusta, Austin. And always asleep before Trenton. One room becomes two. Mama takes in laundry and scrubs the stoops that aren't hers. The world is hers to clean. But she dies before she finishes them all or sees Niagara Falls.

Johan is sent to Aunt Gertie. Me, to Aunt Bess and her blood-stained, aproned husband. Life goes on. Funtz, the Butcher Boy. Learns every cut of meat. Butt, shoulder, rib-eye, shank. Pounding sausage, stuffing casing. Knows who wants what and when and who can pay and who is on account and who will never return. He remembers the egg he stole. Not thievery. No choice. Survival. He and God look the other way.

Every Tuesday Josie comes by for stewing meat. Their eyes hold a second longer with each visit. A good Bavarian girl. They marry at twenty. With a thin, gold loop of a ring stronger than a two-horse rig. On the shortest day. Winter is icumen in. Like now. And four happy years with her. Then widowed. Dear Josie. Josie of the long braids, the deep laugh, and the mangled English she never bothered to learn. But who made more sense than most. Not much else to tell. Too much to remember. Come next summer he sails up the Hudson to get a load of apples with Bert. And never looks back. A short walk from the butcher block to the apple bin. If you don't look back.

Pancake Hollow. Funny name. Syrup Hollow once upon a time. When the maples tapped. Before the buckwheat grew. The old house. Old even then. Older than him, even now. A consolation, being younger than something. Sixty years here in the hollow. Sixty apple blossom seasons. Romes and Cortlands, Empires and Winesaps. Fretting always that the fruit will fall before its time from bugs or wind. Or be pitted useless or nearly so from hail.

He remembers watching a deer on the ridge escape the hunter's scent, but not his. He'd gotten a few good shots in over the years. The butcher works his magic. It's never forgotten. The hart is cleaved.

How many did it feed that fall?

Funtz's sausage, pounded and ground, spiced and cased on his too-long walnut table. He's forgotten just how that table got in there.

Was the old place built around it? Another story lost. Maybe I'll make up something. A good story is not always what's true. A good story is what's remembered.

An old figure, his buttons askew, appears from behind the large boulder. Funtz remembers when he named that rock The Frog's Mouth, jutting out from the hill. The day he posted "No Trespassing" signs to mark his world. Rusted now, brown flakes, only readable within trespassing distance. Walking toward him, a fellow wanderer who probably wandered off the old log road. Odd to see someone up the hill.

Hello.

Hello.

Funtz sees the face approach. Not unknown. Just misplaced. Not from the volunteer fire company. Not from Highland Days. Not from the Strawberry, Tomato or Pickle Festivals. Not from the Penny Socials at the Grange or the covered dish church suppers. But from somewhere. Nearby. A name wafts through his old mail slot.

Haydock, is it?

'Tis. Just doin' my rounds. Ain't seen you in a while, Funtz.

Both men held out their hands, smiled and shook a greeting. It was all they could muster and all that was needed. The old wanderer walked on. Funtz took a deep breath. Warm, like one of those long ago potato field days. Warm for winter. With snow covering all but a few rocks that have been heaving up since the last ice age.

That stack of apple wood is cured by now. That'll burn long and hot and keep Frank warm.

Funtz hadn't seen Frank for a long time either. The last threads of bloodline, but the weave held strong. A few weekends here and there, after the army sent him home. Nasty business over there. Always is. Never a walk in the woods. But at least he came back.

Yes. Frank will take good care of all of this. He'll sort it out. Let it be his time.

Funtz sank into the snow. A feather bed like the one Josie bought. The scent of apples still lingers from the old orchard.

A hickory branch above him shook gently and released a veil of flakes. Some landed on his face and looked like whiskers. The downy woodpecker drummed on one of the last standing apple trunks.

"And All the Contents Within"
a partial list

1.

One House, built 1820s to 1940s
One standing barn
One collapsed barn
One two-story outbuilding
Trees, a stream, a swamp, rocks
Rock walls
One abandoned apple orchard

2.

One porcelain toilet over a hole in the woods
Six weathered baseballs
One barrel, salted herring
Four gallons, Concord grape wine, made during Prohibition
One gallon, sulfuric acid
Five wooden sleds
Three dozen plastic pitchers
Four dozen plastic trays
Eighty-four rotting tires

3.

A hammer
A sickle
Five red flags
Two Red Cross flags
Two dozen American flags
One Marine uniform

Five police nightsticks
One Civil Defense gas mask
One Civil Defense Geiger Counter
Twelve canvas army cots
One box, spent cartridges
One box, clamshells
One box, golf balls
One rusted putter
One number two wood
One dollar bill from the Central Bank of the Bahamas

4.
Two signs, "No Parking"
Two signs, "Park Here"
One sign, "Summer Cottage for Rent"
One sign, "Quinces for Sale"
One sign, "4-H Member"
One portrait of a woman in blue
One girly poster hidden in the woodpile
Five separate woodpiles
Five thousand ladybugs

5.
One flattened cat skeleton
Three deer antlers
Four rusted claw hammers
Three rusted ball peen hammers
Seventeen rusted files
Eight rusted chisels
Three rusted pliers
A wooden handled brace

Two wooden handled screwdrivers
A wooden handled chisel
Eleven yet unidentified tools
One sack that held "Porto Rican Sugar"
Four drums that held "Portuguese Apple Juice"

6.
An 1890s stove
A 1920s stove
A 1930s stove
A 1950s stove, The "Vernois Constellation"
Three refrigerators
The Crosley Shelvador
Two beds without a headboard
Two headboards without a bed
Panes of glass
Panes of isinglass
Window frames without glass
One box, radio tubes
One old radio

7.
One box, "Speedball" Linoleum Cutters,
(The Little Wizards of Artcraft)
One box, "Kleenest" Pipe Filters (Prevents tongue bite
and raw mouth)
One tin, "The same good lamps you use at home—
Edison Mazda Lamps—
for your car!"

One postcard, dated August 9, 1951:
> "Am having a wonderful time. Go swimming
> almost every day.
> Went to the movies twice already.
> Will tell you about it when you write to me."

8.

Mismatched handmade shoes, used as wall insulation
200 gallons of kerosene
Two kerosene house heaters
One hood from a 1940s Oldsmobile
One trunk from a 1940s Oldsmobile
One 1940s New York City Fire Department Utility Wagon
Three license plates

9.

One "Pollyanna" game board
Toy trucks and buses, cars and planes
One toy tractor
Marbles (three cat's eyes)
One streamer trunk with rusted locks
Shards of pots and dishes
One rusted straight razor
One old boot heel
One Ouija Board
One divination wand

10.

Thirty unused Wonderbread bags
Two dozen foil-lined bags from Brook's house of Bar-B-Q
20 pounds of Borax

A ring of 20 rusty keys
A maze of mouse nests
Three screen doors without screens
Three screens that fit nothing
Three orchard smudge pots
One jar Iodex Ointment
Eighteen prune juice jars filled with dated water (12/3/68)
Fifteen volumes, "The Wonderland of Knowledge"
One volume: "United States Coast Pilot—Point Judith to
New York, 1917"

11.
One 1930s ivory satin wedding gown
Two initialed walking sticks, with handles worn smooth

Arrival

When Frank moved into the old farmhouse with all its things, he owned a meager present and had only put down the bare minimum on an unknown future which he predicted would be a cloudy mix of disconnected images, unrequited dreams and stark phantasms stirred up from the inky depths of an unnamed, uncharted sea.

He felt relieved to be able to move into a house that supplied its own past. He felt it would be the perfect time to leave his own behind. The dull, dry dust of his childhood. The choices on his graduation day: Trade School, The Army, or Jail. The years of pickup jobs he couldn't keep, the petty crimes, his hallucinations, sometimes drug-induced but mostly from wandering too far afield inside his own head, the handwriting on the wall: enlist or be found somewhere, barely identifiable. The throw of the dice: the Army. Learning the basics of the basics. The fights, the blame, the near discharge. The Sergeant who took the time to take the time. The crosshair calm, that gift that came almost too late. His sniper's stare. His shipping out. The things he did and didn't do. The things he couldn't do and did. The things he saw. The three he lost. The orderly stress disorder that day by day sat behind and then beside him. Back to stateside. The meds that would or would not kick in. His therapy that he could talk about. The therapy he couldn't. The leaving all he knew for a life he had to find. On his back. In the dark. Staring at the ceiling, sky, or that thing that kept its own silence. And then the phone call. Out of the blue. And then the letter. A Hudson Valley house. A house he'd visited twice as a kid. The place old uncle Funtz lived, his father's eldest uncle. Paper thin. Wiry, they called him. And over 100. And gone now, but left a will. A joke until it wasn't. It all goes to Frank. The next in line. A family line you can't erase, can't blot out, can't cover over. And a new life to piece together. And why not? The old one had been abandoned or had abandoned him. A house, paid for. And with his Army pay, a life could be lived. A new life. In an old house. His past could just fade away, like an old soldier. His past would be what the house would offer. Not *his* past; it was *The* Past. A past that the house would reveal, slowly, layer by layer, when it felt that he was ready. A wave of contentment, a particle of well-being to be caught up in.

For the first time, he began to breathe deep. Not the deep catch breaths from running off and running away that had signatured his life. It was a different breathe now; he might even find a rhythm. Frank slowly began to take it all in, to settle down, like the old house had done when it, too, long ago, understood that this was the place of beginning.

Boundaries

He wondered if that chestnut tree was still there. Marking the edge of his land. The edge of his world. Beyond which lived the wood beyond his world.

And those heaps of stones. Some just left in piles and others heaved into fences. Both looking as permanent as anything could be. And those trees. Many of them, he thought, could have lived three men's lives. Marking the place of beginning.

He'd walk the perimeter tomorrow, to find his boundaries marked by day-glo plastic ribbons tied around trunks. His world now bounded by day-glo ribbons tied around trees.

But where was Haydock Carpenter? And William St. Johns, and Charles Young and Abraham Wooley? Would they ever come to their side of the stone fences, and stop, waiting for an invitation to climb over onto land that wasn't theirs? Would he do the same? Perhaps, out of respect, they'd walk to that place where their fences meet.

He imagined the conversation would start with a greeting, then an introduction and a handshake, and then meander onto weather, mud season, orchards, crops, livestock. And what about that new threshing machine, and that new canal, and those city people we see more and more of.

"And the time is going so fast now, it isn't like it used to be. Back when."

"Nothing's like it used to be."

After a nod, he'd ask what was the best way to straighten out the tines of his pitchfork, and he'd receive, forcefully but respectfully, four differing and definitive answers. And then—that silence that is shared by men. Until words finally break through.

"Well, there's work to do and standing around gabbing like old women isn't getting the buckwheat cut."

Then, as quietly as they'd approached, they'd depart. To tend what needed tending.

Household
Tales
Part 1

The Possessed

The exact phrase in Funtz's last will and testament read "and all the contents therein." The property surrounding these objects included 7.5 acres on which stood the main dwelling, a farmhouse whose foundation was pried from the earth in the 1820s then embellished throughout the decades with add-ons and debatable improvements. A standing barn, once a large two-story structure and now a more humble one-story, made this transition during a winter snowstorm that collapsed most of it into itself and onto Funtz's Chevrolet. The destroyed section of barn, from that day forward called "the down barn," remained a massive sculpture from the rural Outsider Art school as well as a cozy aviary and condominium for regional birds who now had little reason to migrate, small mammals that in another venue would be called rodents, and an array of twining vines and ivies, both poison and benign. After decades of neglect, the edifice came to resemble the master gardener's potting shed behind Sleeping Beauty's castle, if that castle's jail-like tendrils had spread throughout the royal property, as it did here.

What remained, the salvageable part of the barn teetering on drunkard's legs, was winched together by Funtz and friends with heavy link chains, which ran shoulder high along the inside walls and fastened with industrial-sized hooks interlocking at the four corners. This jerry-rigged chain and hook affair had held the remaining barn together for decades like implant hardware in hips and knees. Signs of wear were visible now; chains and hooks rusted by the Hudson Valley climate and leaks now permeated the roof and walls creating numerous holes where both water and sunlight poured through. But despite these age spots, the barn would no doubt outlive the current and countless successive owners.

The land also supported a two-story outbuilding, romantically called by the locals, "The Summerhouse," a whispered nod to Tuscan fantasy. It was nestled into the foot of the hillside and once *was* a summerhouse, fully equipped with electricity, water, a kitchen, a dining area and sleeping rooms. But this was a past long forgotten and one that Frank never knew. When the summerhouse was a true home and in its heyday, its door would open to dozens of friends who'd train up from Brooklyn or the Bronx or down from Albany to spend a summer weekend or longer (some would stay the entire summer) tending the gardens and orchards, cooking up hearty breakfasts, picking too many blackberries, or simply snoozing in hammocks only interrupting their gentle sway to swat a fly with broad-brimmed hats or floral aprons. And always awaiting the dinner bell to gather them around the long, wooden tables with their long, green benches and their mismatched ladder-backed chairs for the best meal ever— until tomorrow's. Corn that if picked more than an hour ago was not considered as sweet. A roast from an animal whose inception, birth, weaning, diet, slaughter and often name was known. The too many zucchini whose culinary incarnations nearly but never quite disguised their identity, with their overabundance placed into baskets the next morning and set at the foot of the driveway with a sign, "Please Take!"

Then the after dinner games would begin: croquet, badminton, horseshoes and bocci, played with seriousness and skill and interspersed with repeated jokes, shared and laughed at as if spoken and heard for the first time. Play continued until dusk announced the sun's departure, which moved them onto the quiet rituals of washing up, one last cigarette or pipe, and whispered goodnights that might softly linger in a hall or doorway, before both child and adult, each in their own way, would softly enter the gates of Little Nemo's Slumberland with thoughts of what the new day would bring.

· · ·

Frank looked up at the old outbuilding, now a weathered box whose identity was lost. A first inspection revealed damp, rotting sills with walls too bad to repair or too good to replace depending upon a contractor's eye and ethic.

Inside, there was an archeological find to rival old Tut's "Wonderful things!" A mausoleum of stoves, beginning with the summer beehive bread oven, its arched stone opening, keystoned with blue floral tile, long predating the summerhouse which was built around it sometime in the mid-19th century. This oven once fed the multitudes: the dwellers, the transients, the fellow travelers, with the extra loaves carted off to barter for fruit and meat, shirt buttons, needles and lace. A great stone edifice to another time when clocks ticked in halftime, when this rural world danced adagio and measured footfalls counted off the rows of pole beans.

Next to the beehive oven stood an 1890s cast iron stove, flaking rust. Every day a little more like earth than stove. And next to it, a 1920s cream and green, on its last legs. Each stove had had its day; each fed a generation or more. And when their end came, they'd become so much a part of it all that they couldn't leave. So here they stayed. Holding memory like heat.

• • •

Frank gently pushed open the broken, one-hinge screen door and left the summerhouse, filled floor to ceiling with boxes, bags and chests, stoves and dining tables. No one alive ever knew what all was there. Did Funtz ever really know? Frank could hear Funtz laughing as the lawyer's secretary typed in the phrase, "and all the contents therein," contents that Frank would begin to examine—starting tomorrow. Stepping from the dark of the summerhouse to the light of the yard, he moved from past to present and looked out to see what else was his.

Trees too many to count and of numerous varieties, a stream, a swamp, rocks, rock walls, built by newcomers who thought they could scratch out a living by farming. And this dream lead them here. To make their dream a reality. Dreamers with dirty hands. The wise and the foolish. People he didn't know, would never know, people who by now had long turned to compost. But in their time, here they stood to make their stand. And with each rock they moved to build a wall another hole opened in the earth to fill with seed or to plant an apple, pear or quince tree. Throughout these woods their legacy lingers: the remains of apple orchards, long abandoned, their last mossy trunks a haven for woodpeckers, those red-headed lumberjacks with axes in their beaks, taking them down year by year. With only a few stumps left to tell their tale.

Frank stood amidst it all. "All the contents therein." And he was owned by all of it.

Possession

The list of what could now be called Frank's earthly goods grew day by day. He started jotting down random items that he saw on the back on an envelope, then continued onto a scrap of paper, then onto to a torn out page, then finally into an old pocket-sized spiral notebook that he found in a kitchen drawer. The list evolved into a piece of cryptic literature, a fragment from a yet unearthed cosmology. Frank's inherited and personal Popol Vuh.

The list notated the things that were left in the house, the barn, the summerhouse and all throughout the property. Objects left to Frank in Funtz's will, objects left unspecified and uncategorized and only defined by that haunting legal phrase: "and all the contents therein."

Objects known and unknown; the familiar and the foreign; the used, forgotten and discarded; the bought and borrowed and never returned; the cat-burglared; objects "stored" for a friend or neighbor; the set aside for future use; the bartered in twos or threes or dozens, in boxes, bales, and chests; the "two-for-one"; the "buy six get one free"; the "you can't have enough of these"; the "better to have a second just in case one breaks"; objects from the "going out of business sale," and the "everything MUST GO sale"; from the church white elephant, the grange penny social, and from the years of foraging through yard sales for those objects of desire, in pursuit of both premeditated and impulsive pleasures with a keen eye and an open mind and the retiree's spare change that burns a hole; the "one man's junk is another man's treasure." It was all there.

A treasure trove of ersatz objets d'art. A wabi sabi warehouse of the rusted, broken, the unwhole and holy. Things quaint and curious. Things tall and small, too big to stack, too short to fit, with names unknown and names forgotten and names made up. Names now in the faded past, known only to retired curators and octogenarian craftsmen. A catchall storehouse from church bazaars, community picnics, veterans' memorials and firemens' parades. Funtz had kept it all. He kept it safe. He was counted on to keep it safe. House as depository, steamer trunk and storage room, closet, attic, bin and box, silo and arsenal. For all that was needed, would be needed, might be needed, tomorrow or the day after that, next week, next month, next year, next Christmas, Easter, Arbor Day. For the next wedding or war, the next armistice, the next event that needed whatever was needed. And whatever was needed was there. There, in the house and barn and summerhouse.

There was never a master list. The master knew the inventory by heart. That mental list of what was what and what was where. Writing it down would only confuse. And all of this, two centuries' worth of what and where and why and for whom finally faded in a whispered litany with Funtz's final breath. And with his death, the glue, the twine, the solder that kept these objects woven into living landscape snapped and frayed and broke. In disconnect.

It was all Frank's now. The burden of inheritance was laid upon his shoulders. Possessions, to sort and separate and stack until exhaustion moved both he and them, en masse, further down life's indelible path.

Taking Stock

Frank drove to the Highland Post Office where if the line was longer than two people, sighing, glancing at watches and general fidgeting ensued. But Frank didn't get farther than the outer lobby. He stood in front of the Community Bulletin Board beside the inner entrance door and scoured the three-by-five foot corkboard for a place to thumbtack his announcement.

"Yard Sale 9–4, Saturday" followed by his address on Pancake Hollow. Black block lettering written on a three-by-five index card. Frank figured that his offering needn't be on a full-sized notebook page. There'd be no room for it; the community bulletin board was nearly always full. He also thought discretion was the better part of the yard sale game. He only wanted those serious players to step up to the plate. And up to the bowls and tools and tables and all the other objects that would be displayed to the curious and obsessed.

He looked at the bulletin board where other events had been tacked, and read three postings to see if his would fit in. Fitting in was part of community life.

Notice One: "Bake Sale this Saturday to benefit Darla Jones Dialysis Treatment. Homebaked goodies, bring one, buy a few!" (details followed)

Notice Two: "Knitting Circle—Looking to finish that project? Gentle instruction for beginners, support for old hands." (details followed)

Notice Three: "Let's talk about Sartre. Mondays, 7 PM. Meet here." (No other details followed.)

He wasn't sure where his announcement would fit in. He didn't want to take Highlanders away from Darla's important quest. There were priorities after all, and he had been on the receiving end of medical compounds long enough to know what was important in life and what wasn't. That mountain of possessions he'd inherited seemed frivolous now in the face of life and death. Buying a coffee cake at the Methodist Church could actually help save a life. Taking away his dozen museum quality Wonderbread bags wouldn't save anything, except perhaps the bags themselves, assuming that they found a more hospitable environment. But hardly what anyone would call a life-changing event.

Then there was the Sartre note. Would he want a gaggle of existentialists rooting around among his things, seeing only the meaninglessness of each item, and only a breath away, like themselves (and Frank), from disintegrating into the oblivion that was the universal and unstoppable future? No. Frank decided that it would probably be better if that crowd stayed away as well.

He also rationalized that he didn't have anything in the upcoming sale that would interest knitters, young *or* old. And he'd have to live through the embarrassment of grey-haired matrons coming and not buying anything, or worse, buying something because they felt sorry for him.

A gush of childhood memory poured through the old pipeline. A pipeline that had been plugged up for years. The lemonade stand set up off the driveway by the mailbox. Ten cents a cup, five cents for refills. After several hours of no lemonade orders, with the ice nearly melted and the evaporation rate doubling then tripling as the sun reached its zenith, and with even the mailman showing no interest, two customers appeared. An aunt, a knitter of socks and mittens, and an uncle, who had bellied up to many a bar for boilermakers before heading home from his day shift at the steel mill. They had dropped by to return a fondue set they'd borrowed for the Methodist Church Supper. Young Frank poured out two cups of his brew, now a bit watery and on the downward slushy slope from cold to warm. His uncle ordered a second (his true colors were showing), and after downing their drinks, the uncle left three quarters on the change plate. The lemonade was ten cents a cup. Three cups. Thirty cents. Seventy-five cents was left. "Keep the change!" An extravagant and pitiful tip, even for a child. Young Franklin knew the business; he just didn't understand the marketplace. Would he understand it now? Or was nothing learned from those childhood lessons?

These layers of embarrassment became the undercurrent running deep below Frank's still waters which at rare moments could turn turbulent, but for the most part flowed on a slow, unrippling course. A course that Frank had created and chosen. A world within, safer and more manageable. This had always been his past. Not like the present he'd been thrust into with a house, a barn, an outbuilding and all of that "contents within."

Frank had never owned things. He'd lived a life of the rented, the borrowed then returned, the found and cast off. Possessions were never part of his universe. He'd never been possessed. By anything or anyone. And now, he owned two centuries of things.

But there were remedies for this disease of ownership. He could go ahead with the yard sale. He would face the public and learn how to wear a public face. He would no longer be the faceless person in the faceless crowd. He now owned things, and things could be let go of. But even against his will, these things began to identify with him. Frank—the man who now lives in that old farm house on Pancake Hollow; the man who moved into old Funtz's place; the man old Funtz left everything to; the man with that collapsed barn, the man with all those rusty tools, the man with those beautiful, old rock walls. Frank, the man who had lived a life with no identity and who never wanted one, now became necklaced with seemingly infinite dogtags.

The burden of holding all these things was too much for someone who had never held anything. He had to let go. He wanted to let it *all* go. He wanted to wish it all away. But the very act of holding these objects in his hands was creating a new Frank, a Frank that had never been. A Frank that Frank had never known.

He turned and almost invisibly retreated from the post office lobby, index card now hidden securely in his back jean pocket. He opened the rusting door to his Toyota pickup and as quietly as possible inserted himself. The pickup cooperated and turned over more quietly than usual, and he headed back to the house.

Possessions. A word he didn't want to speak aloud for fear that merely verbalizing the word would bring even more power to it. The kind of power that Frank had avoided his entire life. Thoughts came in waves to him: Just because a house (and barn and summerhouse) full of things was left to him didn't mean he owned them. That all of this had to be taken care of like a sick, stray cat that wandered into the yard.

Ownership brings with it emotional attachment even when deeply denied and perhaps the more deeply denied, the more the attachment clings and holds. Objects as a myriad of vampires sucking away his life's blood and ultimately making him into one of them. Another object, another piece of clutter clogging up the universe. Without rational purpose, without meaning. Perhaps the existentialists were right. Perhaps he should go to that Monday night Sartre meeting and learn more.

As he drove closer to the house, the thought occurred that he never had to turn into that driveway. He could just keep driving down 44/55, over the mountain. Into another county, another state. He could probably be in the middle of Pennsylvania before he'd need to gas up. The '89 Toyota could still go the distance when it opened up. A vehicle that had never been a possession, but a companion. Even verging on friendship, the way they looked after each other over the years.

Or maybe he could pull in for a quick pitstop. All of his clothes could fit into a small suitcase; he hadn't really moved in yet. He was still eating off paper plates and using plastic forks that he'd found in the house, things that were inherently disposable. Nothing was yet pegging him as owner. He was simply a transient, one of the many since 1820 who used the house as a stopover as they headed West: to the Alleghenies, the Ohio Valley, the Great Plains, the Rockies, the Northwest, Alaska, the one who boarded a tramp steamer, the *Kuela Maru*, bound for the Orient.

He liked his disposable life. He'd lived it since he could remember. Take-out food, books read at libraries. He was leery of getting a library card as that would make him a permanent borrower. Magazines were read in lobbies and offices when his appointments were made. His standing appointment, for years weekly, then later monthly after he was told progress was made, and now every other month afforded him the time to catch up with a variety of periodicals, to be read and then left on tables.

He'd listen to the radio and liked the randomness and surprise of the DJ's selections. He also knew that there were only a number of songs and that sooner or later, each would be repeated. The Western music canon, in every genre, was finite.

Any refrigerator in any apartment where he stayed (he'd lived in a total of twelve in a total of five different cities) only stocked the essentials. And when food was bought, it was bought daily. Leftovers may have made it into the next day's lunch but after that, they were sent away. In the army, he learned that he owned nothing, not even his life. Or anyone else's. He witnessed this firsthand and close up—here, over there and back again. His coldsweat dreams could be conjured up at a moment's notice, even after his regimen of meds.

Frank saw himself, had always seen himself as Mercury, with winged feet. Mercurial in a life ungrounded. He had never seen himself as Atlas, holding the world, or a world made up of the house, the barn, the summerhouse, the stream, the swamp, the long rock walls, the too many trees, "and all the contents therein" on his shoulders. Maybe that "Yard Sale" sign could be changed to "For Sale."

As Frank drove down the two lane blacktop, he saw a sign painted on a flattened-out cardboard box. "Yardsale 1000 feet."

He drove on further. The next sign read, "Yardsale 500 feet."

Four hundred and thirty feet ahead stood another homemade sign, "Yardsale Next driveway Great Stuff."

Frank felt one of his old and familiar anxiety attacks coming on, but he fought through it. He knew what he needed to do. Face his enemy, that world of things and by confronting them, learn their strengths and their weaknesses. He might even pick up some yard sale tips along the way. He pulled the pickup into the driveway. Or perhaps the Toyota brought Frank to this stopping place. There were two other cars off to the side and Frank parked behind the beige Ford pickup that already had two wicker chairs and a carved totem pole in its bed. A long-haired man and his pregnant companion were gently heaving a futon frame over the Ford's fender next to the totem pole as Frank walked past them. The thought came, maybe he should lend a hand, but another thought that he'd be interfering superseded.

He threaded his way through the local bazaar: past the used board games ("only missing 1 piece!") and the wilted children's clothes ("infant and toddler, all washed!"), the two racks of adult clothes, either embarrassingly out of fashion or on the edge of retro-contemporary, depending upon the observer's taste. There were no flannel work shirts so Frank quickly moved on. On to the culinary table, a foreign country to him, lay darkened whisks and chipped measuring cups and one of a kind plates holding one of a kind cups beside one of a kind utensils next to unidentifiable or outdated kitchen appliances with a taped note that read, "Still works!"

Everything was there. A different everything than Frank had inherited but a recognizable universe just the same. A treasure for the person who lived in a one of a kind world where each object was unique and each day dawned anew without memory or personal history. Maybe Frank wasn't so different from these neighbors.

Table upon table of gift items for those in the last stages of dementia where the past is no longer a tangible thing. Mismatched items were the perfect gifts for those who had no past, no life before their constant now that will immediately evaporate, with a shiny new and ethereal now to take its place. The same gift could be given day after day, week after week, with the same response, with the same repetition of thanks. Frank had once thought of doing this when he visited her at the St. Mary's Home, purely as a scientific experiment, of course, but he never did. He would bring flowers on each visit, but they were never the same flowers. It was always a new bouquet placed in the same green glass vase by her bed table, but only after the old bouquet had been discarded, given to the attendant in blue or green attendant garb, and fresh water was poured into the vase. While he was at it, he'd fill up her pink, plastic pitcher with fresh water. Fresh water. It was so little to do. And so much.

Frank understood and even began to admire the mismatched table place settings: the random dinner plate, the oddly shaped salad bowl, a parfait glass from a dim, distant soda fountain when life was a Kinescope. These were the pieces that held the real stories, the deep stories, the stories about unhappy families, each unhappy in their own way. His eye danced over and around these odd, mismatched, one of a kind. Complete place settings for four or eight or twelve carried weight too, but only by the pound. These place settings, totally intact, told the same happy stories of happy families, brought out on holidays or to celebrate a personal milestone: the wedding, the birth, anniversary, graduation, confirmation, bar mitzvah, the returning from war or the far-off journey. The house warming. These complete sets, worth more financially, always seemed to lack an emotional past, held no conflict, held no passion like their orphaned cousins.

Why were none of the pieces of complete sets ever broken? Why wasn't a plate (or two) thrown against the wall in the heat of the argument about adultery, money troubles, moving out, or even about selling these very dishes that had once belonged to a great aunt or grandmother and how, each time a meal was served on them, the other spouse was reminded of the stranglehold his or her in-laws held upon them and how they thought he or she was never good enough and how crashing one of these dishes against the wall would be his or her deeply rooted act of both revenge and liberation?

Frank looked at a red cup. He was always more of a mug person, but the weight and balance felt right in his hand. If I *was* a cup person, he thought, this could be my cup. But he didn't succumb. But the wheels were turning. This is how it starts. Or perhaps it started by turning into the driveway. One doesn't turn into a yard sale driveway because one isn't open to possibilities. The same as the single person entering the bar on a Saturday night. It's about possibilities. Syzygy. The possibility of the planets aligning even if you are unaware that a possibility exists. A man nearly aligns with a red cup. Nearly, but not quite. It's a game of millimeters and nanoseconds.

Frank put the red cup down and continued to wander, eyeing thing after thing. Mundane treasures. Curious curios. The gawdy geegaw. The bibulous and knick-knack. Under one folding table was a cardboard supermarket carton labeled "Stokely's Peas 24 #303 cans."

Peas, Frank thought. To buy in bulk would certainly be cheaper than ShopRite. And he'd always been terrified of entering one of those big consumer warehouses. He didn't need a truckload of peas, but a carton might get him through the winter. That is, *if* he was staying in the old house. Peas weren't his favorite green vegetable; he suddenly remembered the grey, metallic taste from his childhood. But he'd read numerous articles in numerous doctors' offices about the vitamin and mineral benefits of a whole list of vegetables (he was certain peas were included) although all the information merged into one single sentence, "Green vegetables are good for you." That was enough. Frank hated to be bombarded with too much information; supermarket shopping also brought up a crosscurrent of anxiety, so this box that sat before him might have additional benefits.

He bent down and pulled open four cardboard flaps. Not peas. A box mislabeled or else placed to seduce the health-conscious scavenger. Thin, black circular discs, through which transferred sound impulses electronically from cuttings etched into the vinyl surface on the disc from a stylus running over these grooves. The electric impulses converted to sound impulses and were then amplified through speakers, allowing the listener to hear reproductions of various qualities of original sounds that were created live. Recording discs or simply—records.

Frank flipped through the stack and read the jacket covers. The thought didn't enter his mind that he didn't have a machine that could reproduce the sounds embedded on these black wheels, but that didn't seem to matter. The lure of the yard sale had been subliminally implanted.

"Happy Cha Cha Cha by Laurindo Almeida and the Danzaneros"

"The Mills Brothers sing The Beer Barrel Polka"

"Ragtime on the Harpsichord with William Neil Roberts"

"Marais and Miranda—In Person!"

Artists known and remembered. Artists unknown and forgotten. But all had their day and poured out their souls to their adoring fans, their voices now housed in a Stokely's box by the side of the road where fate met the void.

He rifled through to the end of the long-playing hi-fidelity and stereo 33⅓ RPM recordings to the ones with dusty grooves and no jackets. Beyond these, time marched backwards revealing a dozen or so old 78s, labels peeled and faded, surfaces chipped and scratched, but standing tall, defying time and technology.

"Roger Wolfe Kahn and his Hotel Biltmore Orchestra"

"The Camel Walk by the University Six"

"Heifetz, Violin's Genius"

He continued his search, and the last four discs gently called to him as he read their names.

Bumblebee Slim

Peetie Wheatstraw

Hambone Willie Newbern

Leroy Carr

The elder men of the blues before the blues had a name. Here. In a cardboard box under a folding aluminum table. Some of the last pieces of a puzzle left to the world. If the world cared. Frank had heard their names back in one of the cities he'd lived in. He couldn't remember where, but the image of the old black guitarist and mouth harp player sitting on the stoop of a storefront rose up clearly before him. Singing for dollars and dimes, but nodding to nickels and pennies.

He remembered an elderly, black voice that had resonated faintly around him. "Now I'm gonna play a tune from Bumble

Bee. Here's one of Peetie's favorites. I helped Hambone with the bridge on this song. Leroy let me sit in on this one."

Lies? Perhaps. Even probably. But maybe not true lies. Perhaps just scraps of fuzzy details that storytellers weave to help a story live. To help the song sing. Stories are never about what happened or didn't. They're about the truth in the moment of the telling. About how past events connect with the present, and are even more a part of the present.

Frank lifted out the four old blues 78s and cradled them under his arm. He looked around to see who was in charge and his eyes landed on a stout woman in a floral caftan smoking the last of a Lucky Strike.

"How much are these?

"The records, the records are a dollar apiece."

"OK."

The woman looked disappointed. Frank had broken the second rule of yard sale etiquette. (The first rule is to always look uninterested.) He broke the "counter-offer" rule, the rule that states plainly in "An Oral Guide to Yard Sale Etiquette," a book that has never been written but is simply understood by those who frequent these events. There has to be a counter-offer. The price is never the price, but an introduction to an intricate and well-coordinated dance that leads to obtaining the object of desire, or not. This universal dance, not unique to the Hudson Valley, had been played out for millennia, from the souks of Marrakech to the bazaars of Timbuktu. This knowledge of buying and selling traveled the world on foot, by caravan, by cart, by flatboat and sailing ship. One could argue that it was the oldest profession and was most certainly well-established as a part of the world's second oldest.

The conversation should have gone:

"How much?"

"The records are a dollar apiece."

"Even these old ones?"

"I'll give you the whole box for eight dollars."

"They're pretty scratched up. How's a quarter apiece for these?

"You're not gonna find those anywhere else."

"How's fifty cents apiece?"

"Come back at five, if they're still there, fifty cents apiece."

"I've got a thing—I have to be somewhere at five. Can you hold them?"

"Everything left is going to the dump at five."

"I been out all day, I have a buck seventy-five left."

"Make it two bucks and you take 'em home."

"Two bucks sounds fair."

"Deal..."

The two nod. The cash is transferred. Cash money only. The deal is sealed. The records leave the premises. Buyer and seller are happy. But Frank didn't know the banter. He didn't know the dance.

He handed the woman four dollars and with the four old records in hand, he headed back to his truck. Four more cars had nearly hemmed him in, and he had to jockey out of the driveway, nearly hitting a new Lexus.

He had gotten his treasure. With reservations, of course. He had no turntable, no record player, or even an old wind-up Victrola to hear the old gentlemen. But maybe there was one of these machines somewhere in the house. Maybe one was hiding in a musty corner in an upstairs room or in the barn or summerhouse. He thought he'd gone through all of it, but there was so much, things piled floor to ceiling, hidden under the stairs, in cardboard boxes under tables. Perhaps, somewhere on the premises, there was a box that didn't contain peas or creamed corn or Brillo Pads as labeled, but contained the repairable parts of a turntable, a record player, or the supreme treasure: a pristine vintage Edison windup Victrola. And if by chance none of these sound machines were among the "contents therein," then they were out there. Somewhere. There were other yard sales, junk shops, flea markets. It could be his quest. To find a machine that could unleash the raspy voices of Bumble Bee, Peetie, Hambone and Leroy. He owed them that much. He owed it to the world to break their silence.

One Day Only

First, he made a sign. "Yard Sale Today." Very simple. Very generic. That way, he could reuse it tomorrow, or whenever the need to move his wares called out to him. Around dusk the day before, he set up a variety of tables and laid out tarps and ground cloths all over the yard on which the featured pieces would be carefully positioned. Then, after checking the dew point on the weather hotline, he started to move the large objects into place. The maple chest of drawers, the Swedish trunk, the nesting tables, the milking stools, the barrel of salted herring of unknown origin along with a dozen other eye-catching items were rolled out from the back porch. Checking the dew point was perhaps overkill, but it would have added more work if Frank had to wipe the next morning's dampness off of everything. This would cut into his early setup time for the hundreds of smaller items, and he'd lose that final display aesthetic. He'd learned from working retail one Christmas holiday, even through it was only in the stockroom (Frank became too distracted to work the floor after several hours), that the presentation is at least seventy-five percent of the enticement to the buyer. The next twenty percent was considering the purchase price and the final five percent was consumer whim and impulse. Frank was glad that he had taken the department store's one day intensive training session for now that information was coming in handy. But even with this past knowledge, it wasn't enough to stop the initial stirrings of anxiety that always arose when Frank embarked into the unknown.

Frank checked the weather forecast for the fifth time. All was acceptable so he completed Phase One. It took longer than he had expected, but then all things took longer for Frank. Time slipped through his fingers so easily. So quietly.

He retired early, but had a fitful sleep. The dream of a band of thieves kept him restless. With their lights off, two panel trucks silently pulled into the driveway, loaded up everything, even the old paint-spattered ground cloths, and silently sped off. At three a.m. the dream even woke him up, and he peered out the window to see, with the moon's help, the dim silhouettes of his construction, appearing in that ghostly light like a miniature cityscape that had not yet awoken. All was safe. All was in place. This thought eased Frank's mind, allowing a tiny smile that didn't quite emerge onto his lips, but was felt between tongue and teeth. Anxiety and Exhilaration, the two-headed beast that marked his heraldry had always held each other in perfect balance, and this morning was no exception. But a fleeting thought did begin to conjure up before him, and he let it materialize briefly before it evaporated: the thought of looking over the yard from this very window at the end of the day and seeing nothing but patches of flattened crab grass and the gravel driveway dotted with dandelions.

Frank dressed quickly before dawn and made his pot of tea. This along with two PowerBars would sustain him through at least the first few hours of his marathon. He was ready. He'd heard about the Earlybirds, the dawn patrol, who scoured the countryside for bargains. From seemingly out of nowhere, a blitzkrieg of landing, picking through, grabbing, paying and taking off before the owner knew what happened.

He strode out to the yard, checked the large items for dewdrops, which if left standing, could conceivably leave watermarks. There was some moisture, but the weather persons, whoever they were (he'd checked two different radio stations), had been ninety percent reliable, and the dry linen cloth he'd found in an upstairs drawer brought a dry surface to everything. Soon he was uncovering tables and bringing out box after box and thing after thing, and in an hour the field was ready for competition. The starting gun would sound any time now. He only hoped that a crowd, even a small one, would be respectful of the contents. And that the grey-haired knitters and the existential loners would not come and destroy the calm, early morning atmosphere that Frank felt as he walked among the artifacts. He enjoyed this calm, and he enjoyed looking at each separate piece, each with its unique identity and history. He'd owed it all to Funtz the accumulator, Funtz the curator, who knew what each piece was and how it fit together with another piece and what it was used for and what had come along, through progress, the Grim Reaper of Technology, to make it obsolete and forgotten. Forgotten to all except Funtz, the caretaker of this Potter's Field. Was it more than simple objects that were passed down to Frank? Was there a message in these objects that Funtz and the others before him had handed down? From the Saxtons, the Halsteads, the Tompkins, all the way back to the Sellecks? Did each family leave something of themselves behind, creating an unbroken line that would stretch back well beyond what was remembered?

Frank stifled these snowballing thoughts. His task was to move goods in the best mercantile tradition. He looked at a small nesting table on which he placed a rusted hammer crossed with a rusted sickle. On either side were two red pieces of fabric stapled to cut-off broom handles. Perhaps one of the old local Bolsheviks would not only appreciate the display but would like to take it home to complete his

"I miss Communism" shrine, hidden away in a darkened outbuilding and away from prying eyes.

The art aficionado might enjoy the portrait of the unknown woman in blue, stroked and dabbed by a local Cezanne as part of his farmwife series. Another visitor might find the Civil Defense gas mask and Geiger Counter of interest. An item that could be both decorative and functional in these uncertain days. All useful things find use again. The world doesn't change; it only repeats at different tempos.

The sportsperson might enjoy the six vintage baseballs, with finely weathered frayed red stitching, along with the box of gently used but still serviceable golf balls. Included in the lot was an oxidized putter and a classic #2 wood that could still respond to an amateur swing.

Obsessive picnickers or church supper coordinators would collect without hesitation the six dozen plastic pitchers, the eight dozen plastic cafeteria trays, the festive plastic punch bowl set, the seven cartons of plastic forks and spoons, the perfectly useful (with slight spots of mold easily removed) oil cloth runners and place mats, the slightly water damaged stacks of paper napkins and the four gallons of Concord grape wine made during Prohibition if the label was to be believed.

There was something for the patriot concerned with homeland security and with an eye towards creating that local militia: two dozen American flags (50 stars), one dozen American flags (48 stars), twelve folding canvas army cots, an army issue canteen, tent pegs, a box of discharged M1 shell casings, a full Marine uniform, five police night sticks.

And don't forget the children: the 1930s "Pollyanna" gameboard, fading but readable; the molded metal toy planes and cars and trucks and busses, the toy tractor. And the marbles, including three cat's eyes.

For the elder craftsman: two tables filled with tools, known and unknown, used and overused, obsolete and one of a kind. With a loving and knowledgeable hand, all could be restored to their former glory, or they could stay as is as memories of that time when what was built was built to last.

It was all there. All kept safe. In chests and drawers and boxes and bags labeled "just in case." In Funtz's mind, it all would be needed. Eventually. Somewhere down the line. And to every object its time will come again if one waits long enough.

But the question drifted from the back of Frank's brain slowly toward his frontal lobe. Should the collection be broken up? Funtz, as keeper-curator, had seen the value in it all. It was his wealth, wealth measured not in money but in something more. Something deeper.

• • •

7 AM.

8 AM.

No early birds or birds of any feather had landed in the driveway. Frank organized his thoughts as he rearranged the glassware. Perhaps the scavengers had started on the main roads, slowly making their way to the less traveled pathways.

9 AM. Several cars slowed to look, but no one turned in. At 9:16, a blue Bronco swung into the driveway. An older man using an aluminum cane edged his way out and onto the dusty gravel.

"Howdy," he said, scanning the yard.

"Hi," Frank replied.

"Is this a yard sale?"

Frank didn't know how to answer so direct a question. But after a few seconds, he responded. "I guess so."

"Lots of stuff."

Frank kept silent. He felt it was best to let the looker look, then start the banter once an object of desire created more definition to the relationship. The caned seeker eyed it all then made his way to the blonde mahogany coffee table, circa 1955. He picked up an item.

"How much for this old counter?"

"That's a 1961 Civil Defense Geiger Counter."

"Yeah. How much?"

Silence again. Frank hadn't thought about prices. He started to calculate not in dollars, but in value. "You don't see many of those. Pretty rare."

"Yeah, I guess so. Takes me back. How much?"

Frank felt pressed. He looked around the yard. Every object was staring at him, awaiting his decision. Like a photo finish. Like a recount, where the last ballot could tip the fate of nations. Like at the end of one's days, when the good and the bad were weighed out on some celestial scale, and the everlasting final decision was handed down. He had to sit. It was all too much for this transient, this wanderer through the maze of life to make this kind of decision. One that would affect not just one object but would set up a chain reaction that would change the course of "*all* the contents therein." His decision would change the course of history. And is the "Yard Sale" sign just one short step from that house "For Sale" sign, quickly followed by a closing. And soon after, the house and barn and down barn and summerhouse with not a square corner anywhere would be leveled by the wrecking crew who knew their job but nothing of what this piece of the universe held. Didn't understand its connection with all that was, what is and what will forever be. Then some new couple, young, probably city folks, "The New Couple," would build their mansion, thousands of square feet of empty space that could never be filled with the past. Because now there was none. No tradition. No stories. No chests and boxes and drawers and bags filled with those things that connected Issac Saxton to Francis Closky. Filled with all those wondrous wonders that were the puzzle pieces of life and that when fit together, made place and person whole and one.

Frank's top-notch anxiety attack was in full fury now. And his medicine was in his bag in one of the five tiny upstairs bedrooms. He'd have to ride this one out in the best way he could. He remained seated. Why stand up only to fall over? Thankfully, he remembered to start breathing again, something he had been told to do when he remembered he was in the middle of these bouts. And focus. Focus. If he picked up talking where they had left off, perhaps the old man wouldn't even notice.

"Right. That old Geiger Counter. That's forty dollars."

The old man nodded in silence. "I'll give you ten."

In the world of yard sales, where ten dollars is a hundred, this deal should have been closed in an instant. Or perhaps after some minor bartering of twenty before fifteen was agreed upon. But Frank stood his ground, even while seated.

"That's a rare piece. Forty is firm on that."

The caned looker nodded again, smiled, replaced the counter on the blonde mahogany coffee table, tottered back to his Bronco and drove off. Frank had lost a sale, but had set the value on what lay before him.

He took the Geiger Counter inside to the porch and set it by the door. No, this piece wasn't going to sold today, or any other day. Over the course of a few minutes, the Geiger Counter became, once again, something that belonged to the house, and not a separate entity. He headed back to the yard where a green Outback was parked and a young man and woman, mid-thirties perhaps, were weaving through the tarps and tables. After some deep breathing, ten counts in, ten counts out, Frank was ready for the next skirmish. He approached them and the woman asked him if this was a yard sale. He didn't understand why this was the second person to ask such an obvious question, but he was glad that she did.

"Well, yes and no," was his reply. Frank then informed them that a dealer, an antiques dealer, a high-end antiques dealer, from Kingston had just left and had bought the whole lot and that he would be returning with his truck that afternoon to pick it all up.

The couple nodded and the woman said that she was sorry that the Ouija Board was not for sale. She asked if maybe he could sell just one piece. The dealer wouldn't know. It was only one small thing. There was a mild flirtation here as her companion checked the marks on the golf balls. Frank held his ground. He said he wouldn't have a problem letting one piece go, but the dealer had specifically eyeballed that Ouija Board, and that, in fact, was the very item that had clinched the deal. The mask of flirtation dropped to a neutral one. The couple had no reason to doubt Frank's story; it was told with witness-stand conviction.

Even before they were out of the driveway, Frank was carting every treasure, large and small, onto the back porch and downstairs hallway. Within an hour, every piece was back home. Frank rationalized, it was not his place to disrupt the natural order of the universe. His anxiety attack was now a dim memory. He poured a ginger ale into one of the four plastic Mr. Peanut mugs and sat in the midst of his things on one of the mismatched ladder-back chairs. Frank was now another object among objects and the newest that the house would perhaps accept for safekeeping.

• • •

He was not aware of how much time had passed. After certain anxiety attacks, he needed to sit quietly until everything was aligned and in working order. He used to rush his "getting back together time" but now, here on the porch, it felt right to sit quietly until he came around to himself.

When that time came, he thought of one more chore. He walked down to the end of the driveway to bring in the Yard Sale sign that he'd posted. He looked all over, but he didn't see it. He was sure that he had placed it there early that morning. Or late the night before. Or did he place the sign there at all? It didn't matter. It wasn't there. He didn't need it now, and it was one less thing to bring in. Perhaps the wind had blown it away. Maybe someone had taken the sign for their own sale, saving them the time of making one. Frank felt all right about this. If someone needed the sign, he was more than happy to have them take it. And for no cost. That was neighborly. And helpful. And it did fulfill the bottom line of the yard sale motto—"to end with less than you started with."

It had been a good day. And that night, after spending hours finding the proper place for nearly every item, Frank slept well.

Diary
Part 1

Wood and Water

Chop Wood

Carry Water

How romantic they make it sound.
How serene—

But in the heat of day,
when wood and water call you
to the field and battle lines are drawn—
it's they who've come to win the day.

The density of water.
The awkwardness of wood.
The weight of either can kill you
three times over.

Wood and water mean no harm.
It's just their way.

In their stillness
they watch you evaporate,
or become seasoned, ready for the fire.

And even in the sweat of night's splintered sleep,
there is no oneness with wood and water.

There's only the next day's battle
to plan a dozen different ways—
till dawn,
when muster sounds
and battlelines are drawn again.

Chop and Carry.

This is what we do.

This is what we do.

Behind the Barn

Pissing behind the barn
    a convergence of man and time and place.

Falling water arcs a good soak
    a soft and steady rain.

Sinking to an unseen river
    the unnamed source of all secrets.

Merging waters that have touched
    the lips of love, the tongues of bliss.

Meandering ancient fingers
    gloved in rocky veins.

Returning after countless revolutions
    to journey's end, the place of beginning.

Drawing up from deep dug wells
    to restore the parched, the waiting.

Till nature calls him out again,
    behind the barn.

Her Falling Time

She stood with eyes to heavens.
Looking up the gowns of the skygods.
In that time when she was one of many.
A forest of brothers and sisters

digging in and reaching up.
Their only purpose:
to root and bark, and branch;
to sap and twig and leaf.
to move in two directions at once.

> Until her falling time.

The time when she is chosen
among the many.
The time that comes unannounced
but is not unknown.

She knew her time was near.
She'd lost count
of how many seasons she'd passed.
And she no longer trusted her rings
to ring truth.

Bugs and birds, wind and lightning—
whittling and gnawing
layer by layer.
Again and again.

> Until

her digging in and reaching up
ceases.
Her falling time is now.

The Road Long Traveled

Along the road blacktopped and tiger-stripped.
A road that once had been a path for red-skinned traders
their beads and shells long buried.

A road for white-skinned journeymen, moving on
to manifest their destinies.

The old Post Road carrying news of birth and death
to the four corners.

The logging road shaping timber plank and beam
to build the staid and staying.

A road named for the long forgotten hero
who fought to save this patch of ground
for those here now jogging leisurely its length
without memory or destination.

Looking down the road, along its cindered shoulder,
lies a fox, or what once was fox now doornail dead.
Caught in a world we made.

Once russet fur sleek with prideful shine now dusty grey
and scraped away by rough and seething winds.

Crossed bones. Cross-hatched.
An anatomy of neglect.

A head, or what once was head, a skin of thin dry vellum
stretched beyond a thought.
Caught in a world we made.

And somewhere down the road,
I'll turn around and head for home.

And with each step I hear a voice
muttering a selfish prayer—our selfish plea:

Not to end like fox.
Without comfort or understanding or tomorrow.

Paleontology

She flies in slate.
Old bug-winged fossil.

      Landlocked,
      but never landing.

At rest in a sky of stone.

When to Stop
Filling the Feeder

when the chickadees stop flocking?
when the red-winged blackbirds descend?
when the squirrels in their infinite and collective wisdom
learn of latches?
when the bin of seed scrapes bottom?
when spring's bounty that was rumored has burst forth?
when the cat blitzkriegs and victory turns habit?
when bears come out of the woods?
when you leave the house for beachy bungalow or
mountain hideaway?
when feeding birds escapes your list?
when feeding birds is passing memory?
when your shadow no longer crosses the yard?
the one who picked the pears
the one who fed the birds.

tall flowering stalks
by the barn

hollyhocks

the very image of hollyhock

present perfect hollyhock

> or just that thing called hollyhock?
> its name unnamable?

the bees don't know its name
the bees don't care to know
> the bees dance without question

Yard Sale

The debate was whether the tea cozy should be
on the 50 cent table
or the 25 cent table. After a conference in which
all sides were heard,
it was decided that the tea cozy should start
on the 50 cent table
and then, at 3 o'clock, if unsold, should move
to the 25 cent table.
It was also decided that at 5 o'clock, the 50 cent table
becomes the 25 cent table.

The objective is to end with less that you start with.
To see only the table
and not what the table held.
To walk away with a lighter load.
At night, to hit the pillow with less baggage.
And with luck—
you'll sell the table, too.

Goddess of the Vine

Cantaloupes
lay lolling
in the summer grass.

The breasts of Lakshmi
surface
from her milk white bath.

A headdress of wild leaves
coiffed
in braided vines.

Her ripeness
sculpted
by fiery fingers
and
caressed
by countless consorts
who sing her songs.
Songs of Fortune.
Songs of Wealth.

She dances
in perfect balance.
statuesque on the temple door
and
arched
across my earthy bed.

She spills
over the garden walkway.

Her globs of
            orange suns
with seeds enough
                to bring on Vishnu's smile.

Vegetable Recipe

Steam slightly.

>Don't boil till
>they turn
>grey matter.

Brainless
>clueless sludge
till even they
>forget their names and purpose.

And we forget
the taste of sweet soil.

Dead / Squirrel

Lies in the middle of the road. Flat on his back.
Arms outstretched.

There's a blink of reverence. As drivers turn
their wheels around him.
Who wants to wash squirrel guts off hubcaps?

The silent sky opens and the great
red-headed turkey vulture descends.
So close you can count her finger feathers.
She smells the carrion from high above
and circles till it's safe to swoop.

And with one talon thrust she takes up the once was,
now isn't into her grasp and carries it skyward.

Who wouldn't give their eyeteeth for this moment?

To lie on a country road, arms stretched wide,
and in a wink—
that boundary that outlined you—
is gone.

Soaring up off away.
The winged messenger delivering you, the message,
to points unknown.

Leaving behind only the road with its greying asphalt,
its fading white lines,
and its yellow mustard blooming on its shoulder.

November Night Songs

1.
The wind
chimes
the wind chimes.

Aeolian breath.
Serene bel canto.
An ancient song
last to linger.

Sung by the few
over the few
remains
remaining.

2.
The geese are leaving.
      Veni
      Vidi
      Vici

And with cooling nights
their occupation ends.

They sky parade
in perfect V,
honking horns
victorious.

Winging South
with spoils—
fat with stories.

On route
they reminisce
of empire,
campaign
and everlasting glory.

3.
The train wafts in
on whistle wind.
Alive with loco motion.
Keening its song of longing.

A streaming pulse

of what was

what is

will be.

Neighbor Ladies

3 black women over 60,
           pleasantly plump
in wicker rockers
           on a pillared porch.

Playing bid whist.
Laughing with tears
and scolding with smiles.
           Full of tough love.

           And they'd tell us anything
           we'd need to know
if we'd only sit on their steps
and listen.

But we don't.
           We're too busy
           barreling down the road
kicking up dust.

And they've made lemonade
and ginger snaps.
           They won't give us a flat
           when we fly 'round the
bend.
           They'd never put us in that danger.

But sometimes,
           sometimes they do hope
           we'll run out of gas
           within walking distance.

Winter North Wind

wood
      winds
            whirl
                  winds

over
      branches
under
      boughs

filling the hollow

its empty days
now gone

Kale

Harvest has been over for a while now.
Everything is in.
Except the kale.

Herbs hang dry from cellar beams.
Withered greens sleep deep in compost.

Snowquilts cover
beds and boughs and stones.
Except the kale.

The north wind dances.
Memories fade from memory.

You have to close your eyes and concentrate
to bring back that July day—so hot
your lungs heaved like blacksmith bellows.

And now—down that road of days,
cold scissors in gloved hands
snip sturdy green leaves that shouldn't be.
But are.

Household
Tales
Part 2

The Call

The telephone rang. Frank answered on the third ring.

"Hello."

"Hello, it's ok about not going to church this morning."

He paused, "Ok…"

"So we'll still go shopping later?"

"…umm" Frank murmured.

"I need to pick up some more ham salad and I'm nearly out of my coffee milk."

"…umm…I think you might have the wrong number."

"I'm calling my daughter-in-law. Is this Julie?"

"No, ma'am. Sorry."

"Oh, I'm sorry. I musta hit the wrong button."

"That's ok, ma'am."

"No—you don't sound like Julie. I'm sorry, mister. It's mister, isn't it? And do you live in Highland?" the voice inquired.

"Yes, ma'am."

"Well, I do, too, and every Sunday my daughter-in-law, that's Julie, takes me to church, then we go have our breakfast at the diner then we go shopping."

"Sounds like a busy Sunday," Frank replied.

"Well, I don't get out much. But she can't go to church today, and I can't go by myself."

"Well, I think you'll be fine skipping one Sunday. And you'll see Julie later."

"Yes, I will. It's my weekly going out. But here I am going on to a total stranger."

"That's all right. I guess we're neighbors, sort of. Well, you have a good day," Frank said.

"You too, and I'm sorry I dialed the wrong number. These old eyes, you know," the voice chuckled.

"Well, you take care."

"And you, too. Bye now."

"G'bye."

Frank hung up the phone, the third minor task of his morning. He then dawdled through the rest of Sunday morning leaving a dozen projects half-started or half-finished.

There's a fine line between these two and true dawdlers understand the difference. Like the glass half empty or half full, it's all about perception.

For weeks he hadn't been able to do anything of any importance. He was becoming one with the slugs that had taken over the garden. Eating, sleeping, lying awake, resting, dawdling and the occasional shower covered about fifty percent of his days. The other fifty percent was lost or filled doing something not worth remembering.

He finally looked in the fridge, but it was pretty bare. Time to get an order. His parents would never say, "Let's go grocery shopping" or "We better pick up some stuff at the market." Instead they'd say, "We need to get an order." An old Depression era phrase inherited from *their* parents, then passed down to Frank. Part of their legacy, along with a little cash, an old Colt revolver that his father's father had won in a game of straight pool, and a scrapbook of photos of people most of whom were dead before he was born. A thin inheritance compared to what Funtz had bestowed upon him.

This is what he meant by dawdling. He could have been to the store and back by now. But he keep getting stuck in all kinds of things. Family, friends, those still here and those gone or gone missing. And how it all led him to the old farmhouse.

Frank's parents died within three weeks of each other of the same cancer. You don't bond closer than that. That was nearly three years ago. He hadn't seen them much over the last years, and they'd drifted as parents and sons can. But he didn't feel ready to close the book on them yet either. He didn't know what he felt. But he did know they'd be having a good laugh seeing the maze that Frank had found himself in.

But there was shopping to do. Food. The order. The new world order that had fallen into his lap. ShopRite or Stop 'n Shop or Shop 'n Save or Save 'n Spend? They seemed to blend all together. All had hidden treasures and bargains he didn't need along with a full range of impulse items that found their way home through a kind of shopper's kleptomania. The smaller ShopRite, however, wasn't as overwhelming and had the same selection of tabloid newspapers to peruse at the checkout. And the lines were as long as the others so he could kill two birds with one stone. He could extend his workday so he'd feel justified laying around till bedtime. And he could catch up with Elvis, Madonna, Oprah, Michael, along with the newest idols. And a bonus—reading a story about a Jesus or Mary sighting fulfilled his spiritual obligation for the week. He hadn't set foot in a house of worship since long before he'd moved into the old farmhouse. He thought about that wrong number he'd gotten earlier that morning. If the old woman was ok skipping church today, he'd probably be safe, too. And next Sunday was a lifetime away. Anything could happen.

Writing down the order was completed in no time. He inhaled a baloney sandwich and a root beer before he left as a budgetary restraint—he never went food shopping on an empty stomach. Once there, he liked to ponder more exotic cuisine choices, but in the end stuck with what was familiar and unchallenging to his palate. He also didn't find any "must have" snacks in the cholesterol aisle so he was soon heading to the checkout and the tabloids. He pushed his cart behind a woman in black and eyeballed her cart. Everybody does this. It's like looking through a stranger's bookshelves or, if more curious, a medicine cabinet.

Feline flea collars, chicken hearts, rubber gloves, a sympathy card, votive candles, several sprigs of unidentified herbs and a can of Del Monte cling-free peaches. He thought it was interesting that a witch would patronize ShopRite. But she's probably just like other people. A full-time job: a receptionist at Coldwell Real Estate maybe, kids, pets, coven responsibilities, no free time. Getting things done on the fly. Everyone's the same. Just trying to get through it.

He moved on to the tabloids. "The Shroud of Turin Levitates Above Wide-Eyed Worshippers!" He couldn't pass this one up. Besides, it would fulfill his Sunday morning religious obligations while Morgan le Fey was scanned and bagged.

"I saw it right up there in front of us. Like Jesus was flying on one of them magic carpets." An American tourist was interviewed by the tabloid to authenticate the account. Frank thought, Sure, I mean, these stories aren't just made up. He continued reading how the shroud landed safely on top of the Italian tour guide and cured his decade-old arthritic shoulder when he gently felt another shopping cart nudge his butt. He drifted away from the Turin story when he picked up a scrap of conversation behind him.

"…and he was such a nice man, most times people are kinda mean and hang up on you but he talked with me, said it was ok to miss church one week. You see, you're dead wrong about folks sometimes, Julie…"

He waited for a pause, then turned to see two women, one small, and elderly, the other, larger and younger, maybe forty. He broke one of his cardinal rules and spoke up. "Excuse me, but…I think I'm the person you called this morning."

They pieced together the phone call, and the women's suspicion turned to amusement. Phrases like "It's a small world" and "What a coincidence" were repeated, and he found out that the elder, Alice Millen, lived on a road about a mile away from the house he was inhabiting. They exchanged neighborhood chit-chat after Julie decided that Frank was an Ok guy and maybe even a good neighbor. During all this, Frank was scanned and bagged and was soon on his way, nodding a goodbye to the two women.

He walked to an ATM a couple doors away. It took him longer than he thought to press buttons and read screens. No reason, it just did. Like most things these days, even a shopping excursion was in slow motion. When he returned to his pickup, Mrs. Millen and Julie were standing nearby, next to their rusting Chevy Impala. Their left rear tire was nearly flat. They looked like two cats walking around their empty dish at suppertime. Julie had already called her husband, Joe, but he wasn't home yet from his MealsOnWheels run. The flat was their old spare, and they'd have to wait till he got back. He'd bring another tire, and everything would be, as Julie said, "back to normal." Julie was ok with this, but

Mrs. Millen was a little concerned about her coffee milk going bad.

Frank said he could help them out, and he dug around in the truck for the aerosol Fix-A-Flat can that had come with his road repair kit. He worked on their tire slow and steady, and soon it seemed safe enough for them to travel as far as the older woman's home.

As they pulled out, Mrs. Millen rolled down her window and asked if he'd stop by her house later since he lived so close. "We put up some peach-plum preserves, and there's a jar for you. You earned it."

It seemed like a good trade and Julie gave him directions. Mrs. Millen added, "Come by around six, and we might have something else for you." He could see Julie smiling as they pulled away.

The rest of the day's puttering took him to 5:30. He didn't get anything done except put the food away and stack a small pile of newspapers onto a larger pile. It was even hard to do that. It had all been easier once upon a time. Back then. But that was then. Another time. Another Frank. Images kept appearing in front of him, then disappearing like from a magician's slight of hand. Photos that faded in the light until nothing was left but a blank white screen: Frank perched on the hood of the GTO, in his electric blue graduation gown, his hand doing something silly with the tassel; in his tracksuit ready for the marathon; then a montage of him in camouflage, standing with Barry and Gino, and Kyle, who didn't make it back, beside their vehicle just one day before it was no longer anything recognizable; Frank's sandy hair and sandy skin blending into ground and background and sky. The shots kept whizzing past him, and he couldn't hold on. The moment he tried to grab an image it would be gone, and another one would roundhouse in from somewhere else. Hooks, jabs. The occasional sucker punch.

He finally got his shoes back on and found the keys. He thought about not going down the road to the neighbor ladies. But he felt the door close behind him. He heard his own voice inside his head. "Just go, get the damn jam and come back."

The Millen house was a two-story frame, built about 1910, with a yard overgrown with weeds, some blooming, some rambling, others lying in wait. Julie appeared on the front porch, and with a finger to her lips in a "hush" gesture, and led him inside.

The front room was dark, shades pulled, curtains drawn and just one dim lamp on a circular table in the corner. It gave enough light for him to see Mrs. Millen sitting in an old comfy chair covered with a pink and blue crocheted afghan. Julie led Frank to the sofa that smelled of cats and was covered with a star patterned quilt like one his mother had made when he was still living at home. He'd have bet anything that Mrs. Millen was responsible for all the handiwork here. The covered chair and sofa, the small round table with the lamp and the dark blue curtains were the only objects in the room. Mrs. Millen, Julie and Frank, the only people.

Julie gave him another hush sign and left through a curtain leading to another darkened room. Mrs. Millen's eyes were either half open or half closed, half awake or half asleep. Frank thought it best to follow Julie's orders and wait for what came next. Maybe it would be the peach-plum treat, and that would be it. He counted the stars on the quilt and looked at the stitching. It was made by someone who knew what they were doing and had the time to do it.

Julie appeared through the curtained archway. She looked at him then at her mother-in-law. Everything was in place. She then ushered in a young woman in her mid-twenties in a khaki shirt and blue jeans. She put her hands on the young woman's shoulders and led her to the old woman. No one looked in Frank's direction, and he was glad to be the innocent bystander.

"Mother Baum, this is Gloria." Julie motioned for the young woman to kneel or sit at the feet of the elder. "Mother Baum, we have a troubled person here. She lives in Marbletown and came all the way to see you."

The khaki girl let her face fall into her hands. Her sobs were the only sounds in the room. "Gloria, you haf come for help." The voice came from Mrs. Millen. But the accent was foreign and familiar at the same time. German, perhaps Bavarian, a little like Frank's Great Grandmother's. Another faded photo from a crumbling album. She would sit in her bed and crochet delicate lace doilies that looked like spiderwebs as she'd tell his mother her pastry secrets or how to make sauerkraut in the copper washtub.

"Yes, Mother Baum, I got big troubles."

"Come closer, child."

Mother Baum placed one hand on Khaki's shoulder and the other gently on her cheek. She leaned into the girl. They looked like two cats sniffing noses. Words were exchanged, but he couldn't make anything out except a "yes" and a "why." Khaki broke down again, sounding like a three year-old. But then her tears stopped. She caught her breath, recovered her age and hugged Mother Baum. She gushed out a "thank you" as she stood and turned, catching Julie's eye. She might have felt Frank's presence, too, because she hurried out with her hands covering her face. Julie guided her.

Mother Baum looked at Frank. He was looking at someone, not the woman on the phone or the one at the supermarket, but someone else. Someone in the skin and bones of Mrs. Millen. A faint smile finally animated Mother Baum's mask.

"Tank you for doing good by Mrs. Millen. You come back. She bake you a pie."

He'd been on enough job interviews to know that was his cue to exit. He stood and headed for the archway hoping Julie would appear and show him which door was the way out.

"Vait."

He stopped but didn't turn.

"Dat thing dat keeps you up all night. Vill be ok. Put it behind you. They are fine where they are. They know you did da best you could."

Then silence.

Julie peeked through the curtain of the archway. Her hand guided him into what he guessed was the dining room. Heaps of books and papers and folders covered the large table, a sideboard and half a dozen chairs. The legs looked mahogany and all matched so he assumed it was an old dining set. Julie showed him through another archway into the kitchen and handed him a jar of peach-plum preserves. He mumbled a thank you and some other neighborly pleasantry then found the screen door and was hit by the low light of late afternoon.

He didn't remember the drive home. But there he was, in bed, shoes off and an old afghan thrown over him. He hadn't been sleeping much these last months, years even, but now it was all catching up to him.

• • •

A bluejay screeched from a branch of the hemlock. His head felt heavy, but he managed to turn it to the 1940s analog alarm clock on the sagging wicker chair that served as a nightstand.

7:30.

He picked thoughts out of the air. Half an hour's sleep? Jays in the evening? All this light at dusk? The days are getting longer? No—shorter. He took a deeper breath. Tried to stretch. Eyes opened a little more. Morning? It's morning. 7:30 AM. He'd slept for over twelve hours.

He took another breath then sat up. He felt awake. The wakefulness that comes from deep sleep, not the kind one pretends to have after a night of turning wheels and grinding teeth. He looked out into the yard and his to do list started to materialize. New wheels were turning, ones that were well oiled, and that grinding sound was gone.

Start the chicken stock, take down those saplings by the old stone fence, get the mountain of recycling sorted, clear some brush. And then, start on that outdoor stone fireplace. It had fallen in on itself years ago, but he thought it could be saved. All it needed was small rock supports to firm up its sides.

The rocks he kept in the barn could work. There were enough of them. Over the years, his parents, aunts, uncles and other relatives would travel here and there, and they'd ask him what could they bring him back. And being a smart-ass kid he gave them a smart-ass answer: "Bring me a rock." It became the family joke. And even after he was older, the rocks kept coming. And to keep the joke going, he'd label each one, who gave it, from where and when and then keep them in a box. And over the years one box became two then three and four. All were sent over the years to Funtz, who dutifully put them in storage in the back of the barn

"What are you going to do with all those rocks?" they'd ask.

"I don't now. Something."

But first breakfast. That oatmeal with some of that dried fruit would keep him going along with some sturdy tea. Then out to the barn to sort out those rocks. Each one could have a place in that new dry stone hearth. He figured he could have the whole thing done before nightfall. Then tomorrow, if the humidity held, he could have a burn. He could roast some potatoes in the ashes.

Fire

"It started as a kitchen fire. From what we can piece together, some pot holders were sitting on the stove, they caught fire, then they ignited some paper towels, maybe, then the whole place was going up. These old farm houses are like matchboxes."

The volunteer from the Highland Hose Co. moved across the muddy yard from the blonde reporter to gather up his gear and put his ax back into its slot on the Ford pumper. The reporter scribbled down his comments as best as she could remember.

"Panic, then they get disorientated, then finally the smoke gets them." Another volunteer walked past with a coil of hose. He gave her the once over. The blonde reporter never looked up, but she did get both firemen's names.

Julie half sat and half lay on her couch. She'd gotten the phone call before eight and rushed over but returned home within an hour after the body was taken away by the paramedics. She felt so disoriented that she needed the comfort of her own couch to wait for Joe. She needed Joe to tell her what to do next. She felt unfocused and had to say out loud over and over that Alice Millen, Joe's mom—her best friend, her second mother and only mother-in-law—was gone. Dead in a house fire. She felt responsible for everything, but she couldn't let it all hit home until Joe was back. She knew she should have called him on his new mobile phone that was to be used for "emergencies only," but she didn't want him to drive the last leg with that news weighing him down. She couldn't bear the thought of two accidents in one day. His rig must be outside Syracuse by now.

She looked up at the brass wall clock. Alice gave it to them when she decided she didn't need so many clocks, and Julie wanted one for the new living room. The edge of its frame was still dented from when the mover knocked it against the garage door. She remembered swearing at the man, young enough to be her son, but even though Joe said he'd pound out the dent, he never seemed to get around to it. The thought crossed her mind of how some things never change and how other things change so quickly.

Two thirty-five, and it was starting to cloud up. Julie knew the mileage from Syracuse to home and figured out within five minutes when Joe would pull up.

This was the second Sunday she'd missed taking Alice to church. If they had gone to the early service, had breakfast at the diner, then did Alice's grocery shopping, they'd have been home about now. She'd be helping Alice put away her canned goods and pouring the three pound bag of Gold Medal flour into the canister under the cupboard next to the micro that she and Joe had given her last Christmas. Alice said she used it, but Julie knew she preferred the stove. Alice still made brownies for Joe like she did when he was a boy. It was the only thing she baked, but she'd laugh and say she still had to do her "mother thing." The economy jar of Sanka was always open with a plastic bag over it. Alice hated twist-off lids, and she and Julie had spent an afternoon simplifying a lot of things around the kitchen.

There was talk about Alice moving in with Julie and Joe, but Alice wanted her independence. At eighty-two, she joked that they would have to carry her out of that house.

Julie just couldn't face church today. Reverend Taylor was giving the second part of his sermon called "Family Survival: The Role of the Father, Mother and Child." Julie had her fill with Part One. She complained about how narrow Reverend Taylor was with his ideas about family. Julia's two miscarriages over the last three years didn't help her keep an open mind either.

She did have to help her friend, Carrie, prep for Samantha's wedding shower, and since Carrie worked till seven at ShopRite on Saturday nights, they couldn't start decorating Carrie's place till after eight. Between festooning Carrie's living room with crepe paper and laughing over the party favors interspersed with girltalk and an inexpensive Pinot Grigio, Julie knew it would be a late night. Making that early service the next morning wasn't in the cards, so she called Alice before her 10 PM bedtime. Alice understood, and they confirmed a later Sunday lunch and shopping date. Alice was fine with missing a service as long as Julie swung by around noon.

Julie hadn't moved from the couch. She looked at the clock. Within two minutes of the time she calculated, she heard Joe's rig back up into the side driveway.

The Knock

The knock on the door was faint but perceptible. He stood at the stove, a 1950s Vernois Constellation, in the middle of his morning tea ceremony. Tea stew. Four used bags lay in the white custard cup. One from last night's 2 AM insomnia, still a little damp, the other three from the previous day, now dry. One might have been from two days ago, but that memory was lost.

Earl Grey, Lemon Lift, a Red Rose, and a fourth, unknown, missing its dogtags. He called these unknown bags his "X" factor, and they brought a certain anticipation to the ritual. And that was alright. He could handle that. By filling the largest mug, the yellow one, three-quarters full with boiling water, then immersing the four bags which brought the water level nearly to the brim, then watching it all come together for three minutes or so, a good concoction would materialize. Good, but never repeatable. Even if the same combination of bags came together in a future ritual, the taste would be different. One bag would dominate, another would recede. The nose would be original, the finish unique. Sometimes the flavors were inspired while other times they cancelled each other out. Sometimes his taste buds perceived only a dull greyness—a dusty, tannic, sweet and sour, past its prime. But he would drink it anyway. It was the luck of the draw.

The knock on the door sounded louder. One rap, then two, then one. As he turned and headed toward the sound, he thought about the raps. One, then two, then one. A code?

He knew this from his training, but that was another life. Another file drawer closed and locked with a missing key.

Despite the mild wave of anxiety that gurgled up at any door knock, he approached and looked through one of the four glass panes. Standing on one of the rough fieldstones was a brunette, a little shorter than he was, maybe five-six. Late twenties, but would probably admit to her early thirties if conditions were right. He opened the door and eyes met.

"Dis—is Gloria."

He paused. He hadn't heard an opening like that since the back room of McJinny's Bar. One of those pockets of time he was trying to forget. It always intrigued him, the things he remembered that he was trying to forget and the things he'd forgotten that he wanted to remember.

"Donchu remember us?"

He flipped through his internal name to face file. She was familiar, but then again, she wasn't. The face and voice mismatched. A young woman but an elderly voice spoke when the mouth moved. He concentrated hard making his eyebrows slant into a V. Then his left eyebrow arched and his lips constricted to a small O.

The voice continued. "You look in pain. It's good vee come. Vee bring you presents."

Gloria's mouth moved again with the words, but they didn't seem to be coming from her. She raised an arm that held a small brown shopping bag.

"For you."

A beautiful smile broke out on Gloria's face. She thrust the bag forward until it touched his chest. He took hold of one of its paper handles and reached in with the other and pulled out a pint canning jar.

"Peach-plum. My own private stock. I don't give dis to just anyvun." Gloria smiled even broader showing what looked like a newly capped set of teeth—a little too even, a little too white.

The flesh and blood woman standing in front of him was the one he saw at Mrs. Millen's wake, then before at Mrs. Millen's house the evening of the "séance": the woman he'd nicknamed "Khaki." They'd exchanged two-second glances as he left the wake. The other puzzle pieces quickly fell into place. Peach-plum preserves. That accent. The phantom voice could only belong to one person.

"Mother Baum?" Frank realized he hadn't yet spoken.

"So vat do you tink? A step up from Mrs. Millen, ya? She had a lot of mileage on her. I trade her in for a little sporty model. Just call me Mustang Sally! But I do wish my Gloria vould get some new wheels."

Frank began to see the larger picture. There was a rusting three-tone Nissan (four-tone if you counted the rust) next to his pickup. No doubt Mother Baum felt more comfortable leaving the driving to Gloria, a perk when you inhabit another's body.

"Get vit it, Schnookims! After Mrs. Millen flew da coop, I hat to go shoppink. I tink Gloria is a perfect fit."

"Right, sure." The picture was as clear as it was going to get.

"So—here vee are, how 'bout now a little coffee?"

Frank felt he was still wading through deep water. "Right—sure, of course. Come in. I was just making some tea. Come in…both of you…"

The body of Gloria inhabited by the spirit of Mother Baum sat at the kitchen table while Frank made coffee. Gloria's eyes darted all over the room like she was taking inventory.

Frank's anxiety leveled off, and he decided to let the visit unfold. He could decipher all this later. He was just given a jar of peach-plum preserves, a neighborly gesture, and he could take Gloria out in a fair fight if it came to that. But would it be fair? And do you make the rules in your own house when outside rules cross the threshold? Frank knew he was entering a place he didn't want to go, so he stopped and turned around. He'd play it at face value. A neighborly visit.

Gloria's gaze focused on Frank, but he could feel two sets of eyes on him—Gloria's and the eyes behind Gloria's. He concentrated on moving from tea ceremony to coffee ceremony. The kettle was just off the boil, so it didn't take long to make. He measured four teaspoons of coffee into the glass beaker, then poured in the water, stirred it, then inserted the plunger and pushed the grounds to the bottom while the fresh brew filtered through. He reached up into the cupboard and took down two mugs—then put one back. It was coffee for one, he assumed. But then he thought—why assume anything?

He brought out a sugar bowl and poured some milk into a small ceramic pitcher. He took a chance that the milk wasn't off and didn't smell the mouth of the carton when he opened it. He placed the pitcher on the table. He opened the right drawer of the white pine cabinet and took out two cloth napkins. The red ones. He moved to another drawer by the sink and got two teaspoons. From the rack he took two small plates, hand-painted somewhere far away, with crude and colorful flowers. Slowly, piece by piece, the table was set with the little extras that mark hospitality. The ritual of the neighborly visit. Frank couldn't remember the last time he'd done this, but he was glad it all came back. This oasis of caring around a kitchen table. And none of it went unnoticed by the women.

"I can make some toast and we can crack open those preserves." He didn't know why he said "we." Did he mean the "royal we," or were all three parties going to be involved?

Gloria's mouth moved as a feminine finger tapped the lid of the small Mason jar. "Dis is for you. She had her breakfast. Just da coffee vill do fine."

Frank poured the coffee then topped off his own tea mug with some hot water. "Milk? Sugar?"

"A haf a spoon sugar an' a little milk."

Frank hosted but stopped in mid-spoonful. "And what does *she* take?"

Mother Baum parted the glossy lips into a smile, a smile that invited Frank to mirror, which he did without thought. "You silly—dis *is* vhat Gloria takes. But is dis low-fat milk?"

"Two-percent, I think."

Mother Baum leaned in and whispered, trying to keep out of earshot of Gloria. "OK—but next time skim. Vee haf to keep her trim, ya?"

"Makes getting around easier." Their smiles broadened. "So—what brings you here?"

"Gloria brings me here."

It was odd to hear that elderly, cackling laugh burst from a young woman, but Frank fielded the joke and threw back one of his closed mouthed, nearly silent chuckles. The whole room seemed to exhale. Gloria took a sip of coffee and gave Frank her nod of approval. He felt reassured. He'd never really mastered coffee, and it was good to see both women enjoying it.

"It vas goot to see you at Mrs. Millen's vake. Julie liked you dare. She says she is selling da land where her mother's house vas, after they take all da ashes an' char avay. Julie vants all da ashes dumped at *her* house, in da back. She vants to build a garden to the mother there, vit some of da house ash and vhat is left of da burned roof beam. Den, she vill bring her mother's ashes to dat place, out back, an' mix dem all together. They vill be together. Again. Mrs. Millen and her house. Da house vere Julie an' Joe vas married. A nice memory to a mother, ya?"

Frank didn't look up from his mug. Other memories filtered through from those places he never really left, over there and over here. His tea was rusty red with a faint shimmer of oil on the surface. The oil changed colors as he brought the mug closer. He took a long, slow sip. Bergamot, with a hint of lemon. And something else. Something that caught his nose and palate. Peppermint. The "X" factor. All coming together. Never to be repeated. Only to be savored. In this moment. And with luck, remembered. Sometime, somewhere down the road.

He replaced the mug on the table. "Yes, a nice memory to a mother." He looked up. Mother Baum was looking out at him.

"Day say dat Mrs. Millen *vas* her house. They knew each other—inside out. So, maybe dat is da way it should be. Ya?"

"Ya…" Frank relaxed a little more and took another sip. Neighbors at his kitchen table. Neighbors sharing news and jokes and warming drinks. Gifts given and accepted. This could be his life. He thought of his arrival that first day and how hard it was to open the barn door. But with a few well-chosen hammer blows, a little oil and a little practice, the door became a door and ceased to be a wall. He hardly thought about that door anymore. When he needed to get into the barn, he simply took the handle and rolled it open on its track. Sometimes he'd let the door stay open all day to let some fresh air in.

Frank came back. He looked Gloria in the eyes and smiled. She smiled back. Frank wondered if Mother Baum knew where he'd gone. He even wondered if she'd sent him there. They raised their mugs simultaneously and took mirrored sips, then placed the mugs on the blue-checked oilcloth.

"Vould you like to see her breasts?"

Frank paused to make sure he heard it right. "That's ok."

"You should see dem."

"What about her?"

"Vat about her? It's not all about her."

"Maybe she should have a say in this."

"She vants to! I seen her look at you."

"Oh, yeah?"

"All of you—You all keep all your living too much inside.

"Well," Frank drawled, stalling for time, "maybe another time, after we…" He stopped before he added. "Get to know each other better." Mother Baum was drawing out his middle school shyness that had grown over the years into a private wall of silence.

Mother Baum knitted Gloria's brows. "You both are runavays, you know dat? And you—you tink too much! Do, do, do—do, do, do…"

Frank thought she was singing, but then understood this was her mantra for action.

She leaned in again to Frank. "Don't tink. Do! I saw you both at Mrs. Millen's. A year you could take, both of you, to make up your minds. Maybe a lifetime. And who has dat kind of time?"

"You?"

Mother Baum exhaled a raspy smoker's laugh. "You're funny, Schnookims."

"Thanks."

"But you don't have dat kind of time—not yet, and neither does…" Mother Baum blanked. She squinted Gloria's eyes and ran the tip of her tongue over her upper lip, trying to remember.

Frank helped her out. "Gloria."

"Ya, right! Dare's been so many. Do you find her attractive?"

He paused again wondering what his words might activate. Gloria had a look, there was no doubt about that. She had long crossed over the "good looking" line and stood somewhere between "cute" and "pretty." She could easily head into "attractive" territory if she wanted and even make the long and dangerous journey into "beautiful," a land where many lose their way and few are admitted. He thought of Gina, a woman who sculpted her every cell inside and out, believed men's faces were her mirror and that their words held the keys to her kingdom. Gina, who lived on wheat grass and who died of an overdose of herself.

"She has a look," he finally said. This was about as non-committal as he could be.

"Vell—alright den!"

Gloria's hands started to unbutton her white and turquoise blouse. There was a sprig of some herb—tarragon?—on the left breast pocket. Frank let go with a mixture of curiosity and childhood wonder and within seconds he let his objective eye take over.

He would have stopped the event if he could have, but he was caught in two inner circles, one spiritual, one physical. One didn't dominate the other, but together they formed an even stronger bond. Or was he making all this up and just wanted to see Gloria's breasts? He stopped. There were times to analyze one's life, and this wasn't one of them.

The unbuttoning wasn't seductive like he'd seen from the two professionals at Phil Ladrone's beach house, or when Karen, his on-again, off-again girlfriend would stop by after her late shift at "It's You, Baby," a clothing store for career girls by day, club queens by night. Karen had perfected the art of stealing blouses, two at a time, by slipping them over her thin pullovers. She'd stop by and model them for Frank, taking each one off slowly. Sometimes she'd go all the way, but most times she was too tired. She'd say she wanted advice about which blouse was the sexiest so she'd be ready for her Saturday night marathon. He laughed at that the first time, but the second time the joke fell flat. They parted friends but didn't keep in touch after Frank moved out of the city.

"Velcome back!"

Frank realized he'd been conjuring up Karen to keep him out of the present. But the present always pulls you back when you overstay your welcome in the past. Gloria's Mona

Lisa smile locked onto Frank as the last button parted her blouse and she spread it open. Her fingers then concentrated on undoing the front clasp of her bra. Light blue with lace trim. Neither trashy nor conservative, but showed a certain style. She put some thought into it.

"So vhat do you tink?"

Gloria's breasts were—(He never liked making comparisons and didn't want to now. And anyway, these visitors around his kitchen table were about as far away from the action at the Blue Moon Cabaret as anyone could be.) Her breasts were exactly what many would have imagined: smallish, roundish, well-proportioned with all the rest. Beautiful even, in this simple and natural presentation. He studied them and enjoyed the look, but he knew he'd be answering to Mother Baum. He played this hand close to his vest.

"Charming," Frank said.

"Oh, listen to you, Mr. Diplomat." Gloria straightened her spine and shifted her head to half-profile.

It seemed as much an examination as a seduction and Frank made a concerted effort to stop his erection halfway, something he hadn't done since he was charming Arlene Stubinsky behind the after-prom breakfast tent just as Mrs. Baxter, their guidance counselor, was emerging from the nearby Port-O-John.

Gloria's breasts still bore the imprint of the lace trim. Her skin must be soft to hold the impression this long. She moved slightly again, leaning forward with her hands in her lap: an odalisque in the middle of the next pose, awaiting the next request from her artist. She then—

"Jesus Christ! Where the hell am I!? Who the hell are you!?" Gloria's eyelids flickered and this voice proved to be her own. She looked down and hurriedly closed the curtain on Mother's Baum's show. She jumped up and spun around, working the clasp and buttons double-time like a movie that speeds up for comic effect. But no one was laughing.

"Goddam her! This is the third time she's pulled this shit. The first time was in a store in front of the mirrors trying stuff on, the second time was—Why the hell am I telling you this?" She continued arranging herself.

"I don't know. I guess you have to tell somebody."

"Shut up!"

Frank moved away, leaning against the Vernois Constellation, and concentrating on the jar of rubber bands on the shelf above the sink. Gloria finished her buttoning but didn't turn around. She leaned with one hand on the table near her mug, her other hand on her hip.

"So—what happened here? I mean, what happened between us?"

Frank thought he should get the big answers out of the way first. "Nothing. I mean...I guess I looked."

"Yeah, I guess you did."

"It's not like we're strangers—total strangers."

"You know me?"

"I've seen you. Twice. We sort of said hi once."

Gloria turned and looked at Frank. He liked matching her voice with her face now even if he didn't know where she was going.

"Wait a minute. You were at Millen's the last time I was there. And at her wake.

"Yeah, I was."

"I thought you wanted to say something, at the wake, but I knew Baum was lurking around, and I just wanted to get out of there." Gloria ran her fingers through her hair like a comb.

"You want some more coffee or something?"

"Never drink it." She looked down at her half empty mug. "Jeez, this stuff gives me gas. And that bitch started me smokin' again, too. When she comes in, the first thing she does is light up. Makes me feel like a goddam ash tray." Gloria fiddled with her shirtfront and realized she'd buttoned it wrong. She did it over again from the top, not bothering to turn around this time. "Doesn't much matter now, does it?"

"Maybe some tea?"

"I don't need to get any more wired."

"Herb? Or something?"

"I gotta get back."

"Can I drive you?"

"I drove *here*. I mean, I was driving by—She pulled us into your driveway. You know the rest. Better than me."

"Look, why don't you take my phone number? If you need…"

"Yeah…?"

"I don't know, to get out of a jam or something…"

"You mean if she has me dancin' naked at The Blue Moon, you'll come and watch, then take me home."

"OK, Forget it. I'm just trying to help."

She walked past him out the backdoor, then stopped. "I'm sorry. But nobody knows what this is like."

"I guess not."

"And no one's going to."

"Sure."

"I'll be ok. I just need some sleep. I work up at the Kingston Mall," she added as an afterthought.

"Sure, tomorrow'll be…"

"There's no tomorrow. I gotta take care of today. One day at a time. I used to be an…I mean, I am a…I been clean for a long time now. At least she hasn't boozed me up. She knows I'd end it and take her with me."

Frank stood in his doorway. He didn't say a word. He didn't have any.

She walked toward the old Nissan, turning her head slightly. "So thanks for the offer. I know where you are. And thanks for, uh, you know…"

"What?"

"Not doing anything, you know?"

"Oh, right."

She reached for the car door handle. "Ok, then. I'm beat. Being in the ring with that broad is worse than with my ex. But that's another story."

Frank hadn't seen her to her car. He wanted to give her all the space he could. They'd both done enough for one day. He was dog-tired himself and just wanted to run a cold washcloth over his face and fall back into bed. He'd be taking one day at a time, too.

Coming in Second

Frank's only links with the larger time frame were a small, sunburst clock that hung in the kitchen above the Vernois Constellation, a smaller alarm clock on his bedside table and a wristwatch, missing the wristband that he more than often would forget to wind. Near the kitchen's pantry door, thumbtacked to a dried out corkboard was a comic book-sized paper calendar. It marked the dates of both major and minor events: Christmas, Easter, Kwanzaa, Yom Kippur, Hanukkah, New Year's Day (for Western, Islamic and Chinese celebrants), the Beginning of the Hajj, and Bodhi Day. It noted Equinoxes and Solstices for those who revered more ancient worship along with a nod to the birthdays of several political celebrities and the signing of the country's first official document. It also cited May Day and Cinco de Mayo for those who stood ready to awaken any revolutionary fervor that most of the world now considered ancient history.

The calendar had been sent to Frank in an unmarked manila envelope on the first day that he'd received mail at the house, and he thought that this first gift should be given an honored place for daily viewing. It was sent by a radical arborist group somewhere in the Northwest according to the postmark, anonymously since they were unfamiliar to him and Frank assumed, he to them. Included with the calendar was a solicitation for a contribution, but that note, handwritten on dried and pressed interwoven leaves had long turned to compost.

Perhaps the calendar had been sent because someone, somehow had found out that Frank had recently moved into a disheveled farmhouse on seven acres of ungroomed land, by no means the forest primeval or even a hectare of virgin woods, but certainly with enough growth and centuries of decomposition to pique the interest of a group of untamed naturalists.

Frank pondered the calendar with a sharper eye as his tea brewed. Aside from the usual noteworthy days throughout the months, it mentioned days that could be considered sympathetic to the senders' cause, whoever "they" were. Arbor Day, of course. Prevent Forest Fire Day; Endangered Tree Awareness Day; Firewood Moratorium Day; Wed a Tree Day (Frank looked for additional specifics, but found none), and Loggers Inner Guilt and Rehabilitation Week.

Frank thought about each entry and promised himself that he would at least take a silent moment during these special days and look at the trees on his land with a little more consideration. A faint twinge of wonder passed through him when he finally recognized that the calendar was reaching out with a purpose and not simply sent as utilitarian wall decor. Something had started to root deep inside him upon coming to this place, and with time, perhaps a sprout would break through the arid numbness that had marked so much of his life for the years before Uncle Funtz had passed on and with that, passed everything on to him.

He was surrounded by trees, nearly seven acres' worth. Uncle Funtz, who had lived on the homestead for most of his years, had seen so many of them fall, and so many reach their green-jeweled crowns high into the sky. The old ones, the ones who were old when Funtz first came, regarded him as a transient, one of the woodland creatures who would be passing through, here today, gone tomorrow for reasons that they would never know or never cared to know. They would think the same of Frank and the same of the next person who would come to dwell there, and in a tree-eye blink, be gone.

Funtz had, over the last seventy years, sold off nearly half of the acreage he'd originally bought. One parcel for an access road that traveled up what the indigenous population called Illinois Mountain. Anyone living in sight of the Rockies or west of them would simply smile and call it a hill, and any Sherpa Guide would name it, in translation, "a low rise." The other parcel on the north side of the property was sold to a land developer who soon went bust, leaving behind a half-finished foundation for some city dweller's dreamhouse that the land and its unconquerable growth soon worked to reclaim.

This particular morning was braced for a big blow. Layer after layer of darkening clouds steadily marched in from the west, over the foot of the Catskills, then over the Shawangunks, which stood as the forecaster for all weather changes in the area. A cooling breeze accompanied the clouds, first with just a scent of wind, then slowly pulsing through, scurrying leaves and redirecting birds with each expanding exhale.

Frank entered the pathway that led toward the woods where the mottled rays of sunlight were still filtering through. He liked being able to stand outside in the middle of the ever-changing weather patterns, looking off and trying to predict which one would take the lead.

It was probably around seven o'clock in the morning, but he didn't know exactly. He'd given up clock watching in the fog of war which had laid him up for three months, encasing him in a timeless capsule from which he hadn't yet found his way out, even after ten years.

The path had already started to sprout its first spring crop: mustard, wild asters, violets, angel thistle, high clover and that assortment or grasses, both crabby and charitable that made up most of the unwooded land. The idea of a lawn always tickled Frank. He never quite saw himself on his hands and knees with cuticle scissors, manicuring blade after blade and transforming designated plots into putting greens. No, his rolling mounds would always be "the rough" where a wilder Highland game would be played, leading him from hazard to hazard. More like the game of life than the leisurely stroll where it took little thought to stay on course.

The land surrounding Frank had acquired a richness layer by layer over the decades, dark and deep, with a hint of a Tintern Abbey ramble and bowered by faerie rings. The Green Man had passed through here; his presence could be felt. It took Frank back to what he'd read when he first could read. Of tales that spoke old truths that would be left behind when narrower rational minds swept through to clean house and dust the cobwebs from the door. No virgin forest would be safe from them, and what stands now, the oak and ash and elm, the maples, beeches, walnuts, spiny locusts, are generations far removed. Only the oldest retain the faintest memories of what it once was in that other time when time was season.

The path meandered to where it would disappear and then find itself further on. He'd learned the paths from Funtz on several visits when he was a boy, and those memories still held. Frank walked the paths daily now and started to extend those that Funtz had laid down years ago. A bond had been made between a person and a path, and the daily trek along them could unfold without thinking. Without a thought at all, which was where Frank's life had come. And soon, he hoped, and not at all secretly, he'd no longer remember what life was like without these paths.

He turned at the old sugar maple with the broken bough that someday, years from now, would finally fall. The broken bough was now touching the ground, but still sprouting green. And just before the next turn, another blot of color, half hidden by a witch hazel branch, caught his eye. He moved in closer. Orange. An early spring flower? A fungus on the toppled tree? No. Before him lay a limp, deflated balloon. It had probably, in a last gasp, drifted in from somewhere, carried by a nightwind. He hadn't noticed it yesterday, but knew he would have. He picked it up and rolled it over in his fingers. On its wizened surface, purple letters now condensed and read, "He is Coming."

A balloon from somewhere far afield, announcing an arrival, let loose to spread its news, had breathed its last and drifted into these woods and come to rest. This limp orange fish, out of water. A timeless Dali timepiece. Out of time, now a part of the early April woodscape.

But Frank had missed it. The event, come and gone, was yesterday's news. He'd have to continue as best he could. Frank pocketed the limp, latex fragment. He'd learned to pick up all foreign objects that landed from the sky or erupted from the earth or were thrown from passing vehicles in fits of passion, rage or ignorance. And all these gifts from unknown sources were kept in an old wooden milk crate in the barn. And that crate would be Frank's time capsule. He would place it someday in the rafters of the barn for the next tenant to find and to decode just as Frank would do with all that had been left to him.

The path wound around in a great winding oval and soon he was back where he began.

Cat's Paws

I. The Old Cat

At first you see a rock. Then a garbage bag. Your eyes miss it altogether if you scan too quickly. Only after several steps forward do you see a black cat, moving without moving, exhaling life, flattened out on a patch of low grass.

Frank walked up to the cat from behind, then circled around to its side. Instinct took over and the cat broke into a slow-motion, low-tail run settling in on another grassy patch two yards away. He repeated his advances and saw the fight or flee in the old cat's eyes, but the old muscles declined the orders. There were no more dark corners to hide in.

Frank took a closer look. No collar. The old fighter's ears were pierced, not a fashion statement, but from too many scraps over territory, that last morsel, and an occasional midnight tryst. Missing teeth lopsided the mouth edging it with opalescent drool. Zones of grey pink skin where fur had once sprouted were now cracked and scaled. The smell of decay, which had already begun, rose like fog.

There weren't many choices. He could chase the cat into the woods and leave it. He could leave it where it lay. Maybe the snow would come early before the carcass would start to putrefy and it would be out of sight out of mind for a while. He wouldn't have to deal with it till Spring. He'd been putting off a lot till Spring. Maybe the turkey vultures would catch wind of it and after a day of errands he'd return to find it gone. It would just vanish the way road kill does. With only a select few knowing the real story. Maybe the earth would open up and swallow it whole, then leave the land seamless as if nothing had ever happened. Frank thought this might not be a bad way for him to go someday. Maybe an itinerant taxidermist would stop by to leave his card and after a brief conversation, he'd buy the cat for a dollar to make it part of his "Catskill Wildcats Diorama" where cats are stuffed and costumed in 19th century clothes designed by his wife, then posed into favorite Washington Irving characters. He had an opening for a new Rip Van Winkle since dry rot had beheaded his current old trouper.

Frank walked to the back porch and got a cardboard box printed with bold blue letters. Brillo Pads. Inside it he placed a thin, musty pillow that smelled like weather. He knew he'd have a use for things like this someday, so he never threw them out. Just like Funtz, he never threw anything out. He slipped on a pair of worn-out leather gloves, then headed into the yard.

"Don't bite me." Frank spoke a combination prayer, order and business deal. He set the box on the turf and squatted to cat level. Breathing from both was measured now. "Don't bite me. I don't want this to be about me." He tried to make this sound compassionate but realized that his words were selfish.

The old cat sprang forward and ran toward the woodpile. For an instant, death took a backseat and life sat behind the wheel, gunning the engine, shifting from neutral. But at the woodpile, both car and passenger ran out of gas. Breathing was even more labored now, and the old cat let Frank gently clamp the leather gloves around him. One faint kitten mew exhaled with a breath. The old cat was probably glad that no one else was around to hear that. Frank laid him on the pillow in the box. He hadn't been served up this kind of comfort for a long time. Maybe he never had.

· · ·

The village vet was that mix of efficiency and cold sympathy.

"Is this your cat?"

"No."

"Do you know who it belongs to?"

"No."

"How long have you known the cat?"

"…Half an hour…"

"Where did you find the cat?"

Frank thought this was a curious question. Did he find the cat the way a person finds a set of lost keys, those mislaid sunglasses, that folding umbrella shoved away then uncovered while rummaging around for something else? Did he find the cat the way a person seeks the thing they're looking for: gold, a lover, God, that patch of beach that gives the illusion of solitude? Or had the cat found him? Animals do this sort of thing all the time. People do, too, sometimes. You become one of the chosen. Their chosen person. Through something you'll never fully understand.

"I'm sorry, what?"

"Where did you find the cat?"

"In my yard. He must have wondered in from the woods."

"There are two choices."

She mentioned several complex medical tests and their corresponding costs. Then added, "But these might not help him. There's a good chance there's cancer or feline AIDS."

Frank looked at the old cat.

The vet looked at Frank looking at the cat. "The other choice is euthanasia. What would you like to do?"

Frank shifted his gaze to the puppy centerfold calendar then to a cabinet stocked with assorted kitty care products. How much of what she said was professional judgment? How much was personal? Had it already been too long a day for everybody? He'd been in other white rooms where he'd heard this same weighing in of medical information and had seen the eyes of others turn to him for answers he didn't feel he had.

"Well, I guess we should…" He paused, silently running through the choices:

1. Take the cat back to the woods and let nature decide his fate.
2. Put the animal out of its misery.
3. Rid the world of another unwanted life so we can get on with ours.
4. Let the old fellow rest, and maybe after a few pills, he'll be okay.
5. Do whatever *you* think—why are you putting *me* in this position?

Frank thought hard and after a long exhale, opted for the professional response: "Well, I guess euthanasia is what's best under the circumstances." He saw the slightest hint of compassion on the vet's face, the first hint of humanity to break through her clinical mask.

"I think that's best. This old fellow isn't going to get any better. We can do it now." She called for someone named Sally.

"What happens to the cat. I mean after you …"

"It can be cremated." She stated a fee. "Or you can take him home."

Frank noticed the nuance of language. "It" can be cremated, or "you" can take "him" home. It wasn't the first time he'd felt the marketplace manipulate him while his shields were down. What had once been about the cat now became about him and the cat.

"I'll take him home."

"Do you want to stay here or wait in the lobby?"

He'd come this far. No one was kicking him out now. "I'll stay."

Sally, the assistant, entered from another door. She was ready with a small syringe filled with a clear liquid. Maybe it was filled with water and the old cat just needed to be hydrated. Maybe after the injection he'd—

"Sally, do you want to do this one?" The vet put a flat box of rubber gloves on the gurney. Sally took out two and put them on, automatically, while she turned to Frank. "This is my first one."

The vet picked up the old cat and cradled him, stroking his head and ears. The weak but audible drone of a purr rose from deep inside. Sally stepped forward and inserted the small needle between his shoulder blades then slowly plunged in the liquid until there was nothing left. In about five seconds, the old cat let go of his ninth life and lay limp in the arms of the vet. She shifted him into a relaxed pose, his head resting in the crook of her elbow.

"I think we're finished."

"So, I guess that's it."

"You both made the right decision."

"Both?"

"Yes." She laid the old cat out in the Brillo box and told Frank the front desk would take care of everything when he was ready. He mumbled a few phrases that sounded like "thanks" to both the vet and to Sally then headed out the door to the lobby. Sally said something about using the back door, but Frank didn't hear this.

He held the box higher than normal so that a waiting patient, a Siamese, accompanied by a little girl and her mother, wouldn't see inside the box. But as he passed them, the Siamese and the mother exchanged a knowing look. At the front desk, Frank paid the bill in cash. They gave him a discount for some reason he didn't quite follow, and he left.

At the pickup truck, he opened the passenger side door and placed the box on the seat. He closed the door as quietly as he could. The old cat was sleeping soundly. After a rough morning, they both deserved a good rest.

II. Treeman

Dwayne, the tree man, said he'd be over tomorrow. But that was today. Frank finished running a wet wash cloth over his face when he heard a truck door slam in the driveway. He ambled down the worn southern yellow pine staircase to the back door. He now headed instinctually for the back door whenever he heard someone pull up. This was the country, and no one ever came to the front door. No one except those who didn't know better or those who wanted to make that front door impression: Insurance men, Jehovah's Witnesses, out of state Trick-or-Treaters, Toupee Salesmen.

The knock on the back door sounded again, four sharp raps. Frank looked out then opened up. "I'm Dwayne, the tree guy, you left me a message last week." His penetrating green eyes waited for a reply.

"Yeah, right. Thanks for coming."

"Sorry I couldn't make it yesterday. Hope you got my message?"

"Yeah, thanks." Frank didn't remember any message.

"Let me take a look-see and we'll get down to it. I want to stay within your budget. Unless there's more you want done."

Frank had allotted eight hundred dollars from savings for some tree care. Uncle Funtz had let the place go, but Frank knew he could bring it back. But it would have to be done in dribs and drabs, slow and steady, one day at a time. There was comfort here. Frank and the property were on the same journey. Side by side. It felt good to have a companion, and to feel close to another on that journey from the dark woods to wherever they would end up.

"I'm sorry, what did you say?"

Dwayne repeated himself. Frank nodded and said something like "good." Dwayne nodded back and headed for his truck. In no time, he was suiting up near the stand of old maples. "This one here's probably a hundred and fifty years old or so. You got a nice grove of old gentlemen here, still have life in them. Not ready for the wood stove yet."

Frank noticed Dwayne's hands as he was about to glove them. Green-tipped fingers and thumbs, the color of mid-summer leaves, working up past the second knuckle. Black crescents of dirt under each nail. Frank pondered if he should brew up a pot of green tea in the hopes of an in-depth tree discussion after Dwayne finished. Not having an immediate answer he shifted his focus, and Dwayne had turned to buckle on his tool belt. His mini-chainsaw, the length of a sawed-off shotgun, slid into a leather holster off his left hip. An array of cutting and pruning tools jangled from the belt while a shoulder holster housed his pruning sheers. On the back of his olive drab jump suit was an embroidered tree in brilliant foliage, and crafted by someone who had the time and skill to speak from the heart through their fingers. Frank wondered who had created it. Dwayne's mother? His wife? His girlfriend? His boyfriend? Frank realized it didn't much matter. Trees came first in Dwayne's life.

"Well, let me get up there and see what they need. Maybe just a haircut, but I might have to perform a little surgery." Dwayne uncoiled a long length of thick rope and tossed it over a high, sturdy limb. Then, adjusting his boot cleats, he scurried up the trunk of the first old gentleman until he was twenty feet above the ground. Frank watched him prune and shape and sculpt, cutting through boughs and limbs and twigs like soft butter.

As he worked from tree to tree, Dwayne whistled a melody unknown to Frank. Not that Frank knew many songs or had any sort of pitch to even repeat notes. But he had a gut feeling about it. It sounded old and from someplace far away. A hymn or a dirge. An old arborist's work song only whistled now because the words, once etched on birch or burnt into poplar, had long turned to mulch. But old melodies remain in the air. They lie in wait for their time to come again. To infect that special someone who understands that ancient and forbidden knowledge. The only knowledge worth knowing.

"They look pretty good up there. Do you want the chips or should I cart them away?" Dwayne was standing next to Frank.

"Oh, yeah—sure. You can pile the chips by the barn, I'll use them for something." The thought had never crossed Frank's mind that something from the property would ever leave the property.

"And another thing. I'm not sure when you'll want to deal with this." Dwayne walked almost due north to a two-story outbuilding, nicknamed "the summerhouse." "You see this big maple over here?" Dwayne ran his hand over the trunk of the old tree which stood inches away from the lop-sided door. He paused, then spoke something Frank couldn't catch. For almost a minute, his green eyes opened and closed slowly. The sweat from the work and the heat of the day glistened down his face and neck and cast a greenish tint to his skin. Green like the water reflecting algae in a stream.

"This tree's uprooting that outbuilding. I can get you some people to jack up that building and move the whole thing back. They'll have to dig you a new foundation, a shallow one so we don't sever the main roots here. It's an expense, but that way, this maple won't suffer any more trauma."

Frank thought before he spoke. Don't cut down the tree, move the building. Why didn't I think of that.

"Well, let me think about that, Dwayne."

"Sure, you just say the word."

Dwayne finished up, leaving a good mound of chips next to the barn. With the work finished, Frank wrote a check, to the penny of Dwayne's estimate, and he was off, leaving Frank in the driveway. He turned a three-sixty, eye-balling the mound of chips, the traumatized maple, the oppressive two-story outbuilding, and the stand of old gentlemen, looking dapper in their new haircuts. If time would just stand still, everything would be all right, thought Frank. But as soon as he thought this, that thought had already slipped into the past. Maybe some tea stew would ease him into the late afternoon. He walked toward the back door, his hand about to touch the doorknob—

The cat—Oh, my God, the cat—the dead cat. How could he have forgotten it? In the Brillo box on the front seat of the pickup truck, waiting patiently for Frank to create some kind of ritual somewhere on the property. He walked to his truck and opened the door. Oddly, there was no smell, even with the windows up. It had only been a few hours since he'd brought it back. Or was it yesterday? Or two days? Frank decided quickly that the cat was more important than reviewing his internal clock. He carried the Brillo box with the old cat and set it by the barn door.

III. A Hole in the Ground

Frank slid the barn door open, which brought the interior up to a grey half-light, even on this cloudless midday. The barn had no electricity but a snake's nest of crossed and looping cables showed off its former life when it was a socialized building with a soul and not just an oversized storage crate like it was now.

Frank knew he'd have to bring the barn back someday. It was on his master to do list which now extended to three pages of a quarto-sized notebook, complete with a 1948 calendar on the back cover, one of the treasures he'd found in the old Swedish trunk on the porch.

Frank knew the barn well enough now to maneuver in the half-light. This made him smile. Bringing electricity into this place now dropped a few notches on that to do list. He smiled again. He walked to the tool wall and pondered his choice of weapons, like a gladiator figuring what would help him walk out of the arena alive that afternoon: sword and shield, net and trident? He chose spade and mattock, but added a little insurance with a crowbar and garden trowel. Frank was beginning to know the land, its strengths and weaknesses. And his opponent was learning Frank's.

The hole would be dug up by the treeline where extended families of stones and rock slept beneath thin green and brown blankets. Anywhere on the property, it only took two mattock swings to strike stone.

Frank got up to the treeline and looked for a good spot. A sweet spot that wouldn't take him all afternoon to dig. He decided that the hole could be anywhere across a ten foot-wide spread. From here, he could see it from the kitchen window when he washed his dishes or ate that quick lunch over the sink. He wondered why he needed to see the old cat's burial ground from the house. Was he growing a little too attached to this thing that was no longer living? Or was it because he'd never lived close to anybody's resting place?

Stroke one. Frank brought the mattock down with all his strength. It dug in about two inches then hit stone, sounding a sharp clink. The wooden handle shuddered. Frank's arms quivered up to his shoulders like he was in one of those cartoons he'd seen as a kid. The second mattock stroke was the same. The third found the rock's edge. Frank could win the day, but it was going to be a long afternoon.

If there had been no ice age, that hole would have been dug in a few minutes. But big and little offspring from the top of Illinois Mountain had hitched a ride when the ice carved its way down the slope. Those rocks were probably hoping to make it somewhere warm and sunny: the Gulf Coast, the Keys; but when the ice shelf ran out of gas, this tumble of stone had to be content to live out its days at Pancake Hollow.

After two hours of work, with mattock, spade, crowbar and trowel, the two-foot by three-foot by two-foot hole was ready. Hole. Not grave. But not a pit either. Frank looked into the negative space. Where earth had been. Holes are unnatural, he thought. Always longing to be filled. Holes in earth. Holes in hearts. Janice Konich. He thought about how their brief relationship was solely based on sex. They'd hardly be together five minutes before they were inside each other. Filling holes. But it didn't last long. Who could sustain that? Not even the Universe. They exploded from each other one night. Creating two more holes. Longing to be filled.

Frank knew he was stalling. He watched his hands slowly offer the cat into the hole, nesting him on a bed of earth. All of the rocks, even the chickpea-sized ones had been gleaned away, leaving the sides and bottom with a cool, velvet feel. The smell of good earth was in the air, too.

Should I cover the cat with a cloth? Let's not make too much out of this. The sooner the old cat turns to earth, the better.

Why are we so obsessed with air-tight, water-tight hermetically sealed boxes? Why do the living keep us from becoming earth? Frank didn't have an answer, so he took up a small handful of dirt and tossed it over the old cat. He didn't seem to mind, so Frank assumed he was doing the right thing. He lobbed in another larger handful, then a third and a fourth. Soon, only the old cat's sleeping head lay uncovered on a pillow of soft earth.

Frank took in a breath and held it. He scooped up another handful of earth and gently sprinkled it down on the old cat's face until it faded from view. Soon a small mound arced over the ground, and Frank tamped the earth down to a solid mass, trying to leave as little evidence as possible. This was still *his* property, and unwanted visitors of any kind weren't welcome.

Frank gathered up his tools and walked back to the barn. He glanced over his shoulder at what a few minutes ago was negative space. A hole. But now it was filled and smoothed. And positive. Positive, but unfinished.

"I guess you need some sort of marker," he spoke out loud. He couldn't say "headstone" even though this was the first word that came to him. He scanned full circle, looking for what could work.

IV. The Stone

Several weeks earlier, a pair of workmen had come, and started to dig out rocks. Hercules and Sisyphus, the movers of stone. Moving them from one part of the property to another so ground could be leveled, plantings started, and there could be one place without a stone foundation.

The two men understood mass and weight. The density of solid earthrock, and what it's like to stay under that kind of pressure for so long.

One of the brawny lads walked up to Frank. He held a stone, the size of a dinosaur egg or Goliath's skull, speckled white and black and smoothly rippled. Less than animal, but more than mineral.

"See this one here?" the workman asked.

"Yeah."

"This one here's what we call—a niggerhead."

A gust of old, stale air hit Frank in the face. "Why's that?"

"Beause these ones will come right back at you. You can try to break 'em, but you can't. Slam 'em with a sledge hammer, and it'll bounce right off. On to your foot, up into your face. I seen it happen. Knocked one guy clean out."

There was a compliment hidden here. And if one searched, maybe even some old-boy respect. One thing was for sure, that old stone was older than all the others they'd seen. It knew more and was closer to the starting line when the first race began.

All that was weeks ago, but Frank was glad he'd remembered it. That rounded stone would be the stone to mark the old cat's...Grave. This would be the headstone for the old cat's grave. It all came together and when it did, Frank accepted it without any voice of protest. Dinosaur egg, Goliath's skull. Niggerhead. It wasn't any of these anymore. Now, it would mark a life. For a long time. Or until it became something else.

Frank carried the stone to the mound, to the place of beginning, and laid it at the head to mark the grave. The day's work was then finished. Frank could now spend the late afternoon on the front porch with a beer, watching life pass by. Cars and tractors, motorcycles and farm equipment, and maybe that pretty jogger would be out today.

V. The Rolling Stone

The next morning, Frank waited for his lemon, mint, Darjeeling to brew. From the kitchen window, he scanned the landscape with all its perfect imperfections: leafless twigs, twigless leaves, random boughs felled and scattered from last night's wind, the heaving rocks, the sighing barn, shadows of substance. The deer hadn't found the Asiatic lilies yet. More clover had flowered in the dawn dew and in the mottled sunlight, the land turned to impressionist canvas.

His eye trailed to the right. The old cat's gravestone no longer lined up between the dead pine and the sugar maple, and loose dirt was mounded on either side. Frank finished a long sip, then placed his cup on the griddle cover of the Vernois Constellation, slipped on his garden boots and headed out.

The stone had shifted off its mark, and what was yesterday's tamped-down earth had been dug up and scattered beside the displaced stone. He peered into what was now a freshly dug hole and found the old cat gone. Exhumed. Frank felt violated. This was his land. He used his tools to dig into his soil. He moved his rocks. He chose the headstone. He surveyed the site so he could eyeball it from his kitchen window every morning. Someone had stolen his cat.

Frank created a list of suspects as he circled the crime scene. There were rumors of a pack of wild dogs who roamed the area. There were sightings of coyotes high up on the ridges. Many had sworn they heard their full moon song cycle. Foxes were so abundant that when one turned roadkill it ceased to be a topic of conversation at the Sister's Store. The myth of the Catskill Pumas was still brought out to titillate vacationers. And he didn't forget the ever present turkey vultures who circled and soared, keeping both the living and the dead under surveillance. It could have been the resident skunk, a bizarre creature all white from head to tail. Frank remembered the first time he saw it, looking like the animated wig of George Washington, ambling across the yard. It could have dug for grubs, which opened the way for others.

Maybe they were all working together. Maybe they figured out if they'd cooperate instead of compete, they'd all survive. Times were tough all over. Like at the African watering hole where they all bought rounds for each other before getting on with the business of the day.

Frank didn't disturb anything around the new hole. He thought of calling the Lloyd Police, but then, what would he tell them? He'd keep the hole open for a while, to ponder over. It was still sacred ground. And it was his.

He headed back to the house. His tea was probably cool now, but he never emptied a cup down the sink. He never reheated it either. He drank from his mug until it was empty. Only then would he think about a refill. He'd work somewhere else for the rest of the day, somewhere away from the hole in the ground. He hadn't cleared pathways on the northside for a while, and that would give him time to think it all over.

VI. The Window

That night, Frank lay naked on his bed, coverless, with the heat of the upper bedroom nestled around him like a thick down quilt. Uncle Funtz had never owned an air conditioner. He was suspicious of them. Suspicious of making the air around him into something else. He never said anything more about it, and would let the subject drop if it ever came up. Frank was remembering this when the heat woke him, but he continued to lie there. He couldn't gather the strength to get up and drag a sheet and pillow downstairs to the couch where it would be a few degrees cooler. Finally, near dawn, he started to sleep soundly. He knew he was asleep because of the dream he was having. It was about The Green Man, and talking trees. He couldn't make out their words, but he knew they were talking about him. Then he dreamed about all the things that were left to him when he took over the house. Most of the stuff from people he never knew. Were they simply forgotten pieces of property? Or was each item the legacy of those who had nothing else to give, but had to give something before they moved on.

Those old shoes found between the walls when he was patching a hole where the plaster had fallen in. A man's and a woman's shoe. Handmade and sturdy. The uppers were still good. The celebration of a wedding night in the first home of their own. The shoes of grandparents, the last shoes they wore, before breathing their last in one of the upper rooms. Perhaps the room where Frank now lay. Sweating.

All this stirred him awake, with dreams still playing tag inside his head. He heard the low whirring of his small rotary fan on the dresser. He looked at his bedside clock. 6:38. A rooster crowed several neighbors away.

A skim of sweat stuck Frank to the sheet and to himself. He slowly pried loose. Index fingers rubbed encrusted eyelids, Eye slits became ovals. The low whirring continued. Hands brushed through hair. Back arched slightly, then hinged at the hips, sitting Frank upright. Head tilted back, then forward, then straight. Sunlight colored the top of the ridge. The black cat at the foot of the bed purred loudly and began to stretch.

Frank moved from semi-comatose to orange alert. The cat gave him a sidelong glance, then started bathing.

"So...How'd you get here?" Frank half-expected an answer, but none was given. He reached down, slowly, to touch the animal who seemed content to be a bunkmate. A stroking of the cat's head proved two things: first, the cat did exist and second, he liked the attention. He rolled onto his side revealing a white puff of fur on his chest and a lack of a collar. He'd have to think about this.

Frank rose and headed for the bathroom. He turned around to look back. No cat was on the bed. He looked down, and the

126

cat was at his feet. He continued into the bathroom. The cat followed, making a mental note of the man's morning ritual: Frank stood in front of a large, white bowl and emptied his bladder; he splashed his face with water, cold then hot; he shook a small metal can out of which spurted a white foam, which he spread over his face; then with a metal stick, he scraped off the white foam and flushed it down the other big, white bowl; he patted his face with a yellow cloth then took a small-handled brush and ran it around his mouth. It all seemed very complicated to the cat, but having seen other humans, he knew that humans did not lead simple lives.

"Still here?" Frank finished up, then walked down the worn steps. The cat followed. He turned into the kitchen, the cat at his heels. The cat understood that the kitchen was the heart of this home, a thing that Frank was still learning. The cat lay down in the middle of the floor. There would be no evading or ignoring him now. The cat had chosen. The deal was sealed.

Frank looked at the open window on the kitchen's south wall. The screen had popped out or fallen out during the night. Or maybe this was the work of a cat burglar. The kind of person who forces entry, not to steal from you, but to deposit a cat into your personal space, then leave without a trace. And by morning, this gift from an unknown source soon becomes at one with your home in a way that you will never be. And it's a little surprised that you–Who are you?– are sharing space with it. But a cat will put up with a lot within its territory. Even you.

Frank found a little cooked chicken, put it in a cracked dish that had recently held vintage matchbooks and set it on the floor next to the stove. He placed a small pan of water beside the dish. A new morning ritual was complete.

Looking out the window over the sink, he scanned up to the treeline. The stone was still off its mark and brown patches of earth lay scattered around it. Frank put on his yard boots and walked up the rise. The hole was still a hole.

The new cat, no more than a year old, created his own agenda as the day progressed: sleeping, bathing, stretching and staring out at something unperceivable to anyone else except another cat. Twice, Frank saw the new cat on the back porch bench, stretched along the windowsill and looking up to the headstone and the open grave, sniffing the air. When the new cat saw Frank looking at him, he jumped off and brushed against Frank's pant leg. Neither of them said anything.

Frank didn't understand any of this, and he wasn't going to waste a work day conjuring up a scenario that would only lead to a dead end. He only knew what he knew. The old cat was gone and a new cat had come. In through the window. In the dead of night.

Diary
Part 2

Landscape With Barn

For a century and a half, the barn stood. With its square forged nails and foot-wide planks. Knowing its use, its needs, how to deal with wind and rain, drought and snowdrift, and those who burrowed and those who bored. It understood each season, knew its longitude and latitude.

It knew its owners, long and short term. Where they came from, who they were and what they were. The farmers, stonecutters, merchants, and machinists; the isolationists, the saber-rattlers, the racists, the tolerants, the country mice and city mice; the ones whose dreams were fulfilled and the ones whose dreams were broken. The barn saw Death pass over and saw Death visit. It observed the births of calves and kids, both goat and human. It hid young lovers in its hayloft, and turned a blind eye to the child smokers who rolled their own and the old time whiskey buffs who slept it off. It hid a girly magazine or two in its bins and watched a tornado uproot an old friend, a maple older than itself, on a blustery September morning. It witnessed newlyweds leave to build their own barns down the road and bid farewell to a proud few, off to war to save the Union or the world.

The barn was trusted to hold and store, seed for spring and harvest for winter. It was trusted to shelter Abe and George who pulled the wagon, and Flower who gave the milk. And with repairs: three new doors and four new roofs, new boards here and there brushed with leftover paint, the old barn weathered, standing in and outside time.

• • •

The old barn is collapsing into itself. Imploding in slow motion. The landscape changes. Roof and earth are touching points. A point of no return. Listing in gravity's wind.

After a discussion and a master plan, neighbors rev their backhoe and roll it in. With bucket and claw they disassemble, and in half a day what has stood longer than a century is gone.

Hand hewn posts and beams, barn red novelty siding, a coil of unbraided rope, the discus of a rusted harrow. Anyone could pick up these pieces like ocean shells and hold them to their ears. The ancient sounds are faint but clear: the hoisting of fresh hay bales, the squeal of pulleys wanting oil, the lowing moo at milking time.

Two other neighbors take over like carpenter ants to pry off each plank and extract the square forged nails to keep as tokens of the day. They divide what lay in heaps and haul it to the dumpster to cart away and bury at the landfill.

Other pieces, what can be saved, are carried to another outbuilding and neatly stacked against the wall. To be reclaimed at some future time or in some future life, to make a present of their past.

The presence of the barn, though, still remains, like a leg separated from the body, but still felt. And on a foggy day, still seen.

No trace is left of beams and posts, forged nails, handles, angle irons, and runners. What stands there is a Ghost Barn without structure or shadow. A Barn removed, but unreceded. Encased in memory, indivisible and perhaps now more clearly seen by those no longer here. When Barn and They stood side by side, both in the season of their prime.

Shards

During spring melt, the earth heaves up her lost treasures. They surface piece by piece from where they've lain for years. Broken bits of bottle glass: amber, green and blue. One of a kind, made one by one by hands and fire. Wafers of rusted metal, parts of parts from parts unknown worn smooth or rough through working wear. Unfixable or replaced by what-came-next.

Up the rise at the treeline lies a potter's field of shards the size of cameos. China, fine and everyday, plates and platters, cups and saucers, kegs for beer and sauerkraut and a dozen different handles that attached to something, now long gone. Pieces of pots, thrown and then thrown out for reasons now unknown.

A shard of mystery. All that's left of an old, white plate, Italian perhaps, with a delicate flower, orange, hand-painted on a single stem. The wedding china of new arrivals, from which they ate their nuptial cake then served ten thousand meals.

Past Perfect

The back room of the gallery commemorated all that small town America could be. The objects, people and events that shaped the Highland hamlet. As far back as memory would serve.

In this small room, Time encapsulated. Photo after fading photo of stiffly posed Highlanders. Row on row like dried poppies. Portraits of a once-was time and place. Stalwarts of the community who had done their part to keep their neighbors safe for democracy, from bankruptcy, from becoming the abusers or the abused, from the brink of madness and on the path of faith. Known by those who knew them.

Further on, under pinspots of light and placed with white-glove care, the remnants of yesterday's progress:

the frozen clock from the feed and grain,

the oak school desk with inkwell hole and penknived myths,

obscure and obsolete tools once worked by anonymous hands for an unknown job no longer needing done.

And in a far corner, under a lamp with a cock-eyed shade, a hand-written sign explained the object that rested on the floor beside it:

push mower
use by the Highland Hose Co.
to mow the little patch of grass
by the old fire house

Oktoberfest

At dusk, he fills a custard cup with beer. He pours the beer without a head. It's always flat. The cheapest brew. Whatever stray cans are left discounted at the drive-up, drive-thru beverage store.

He places the beer-filled custard cup in the garden. Beneath the rambling nasturtiums, beside the eager daisies, or hidden between the legs of the pompous hydrangea. Almost anywhere would do. Placed like a Christmas treat on the mantelpiece for the after-hour's visitor.

He wonders, will they come tonight? Out of the ground. Out of the night. But once he's back inside, the mission is forgotten. He loses himself as he does so many nights in dog-eared books and old movies, colorless with age.

In the morning, after the kettle boils and the tea has steeped, he opens the back door and ventures forth. To see what's burst forth from moonlight.

And there, beneath, beside, between the bushy mat of green, the cup sits in silent afterthought. And inside the cup, three inebriated slugs lie belly up. With x's for eyes and the slightest smiles curving upwards on their slight slug lips. They float effortlessly in malt and hops, no longer straining for that extra inch from gravity's forced march.

He bends down for a closer look. Who were they really, these small and slimy cousins, rubber-bodied, trailing mucous? Were they, in another time and place: dictator, president, general, lawyer, judge, talk show host, death squad leader, CEO, child soldier—then fallen? Was this their starting over? And was he inadvertently boosting them up the next rung of the eternal ladder? That mobius strip, without beginning or end? Moving them up to millipede, or beetle or arachnid? Or whatever would be next. Was he preparing them for their great leap forward?

Did this make him the gate-keeper? The keeper of keys? The one who unlocks the door? Who machetes the jungle path so they can pass? Was he the one who pours and offers the cup of salvation?

Or was he helping to cleanse the cosmos of what was never meant to be? Something that escaped from the box? One of God's mistake, now enlisted in the Devil's Brigade? The ones meant to be sealed and hidden away? Or is he the defender of all that's good? The defender of the faith and faithful?

Was he only an impediment, the thing to pass around or through? A minor roadblock on the eternal highway? Were they part of what had always been and would always be long after he'd gone?

Or was he simply taking life? The act that's now our expertise, without thought or guilt or feeling. An act to be intellectualized away. Another final solution, dispensed with the washing of hands.

Or was he all of the above? Or none of these? Or something else? Was he the one who asks the questions for which there are no answers? Or will answers finally come? When he's ready to receive them? Which is not today, standing in the morning light, at the edge of the garden, looking down at a custard cup of stale, flat beer that drew three slugs to drink their fill.

Jimmy's Lament

He comes once a month to help with clearing. He spoke one time.

I chainsawed an old dead pine the other day, and carried it down the hill to my burnpile. And when I threw that log over my shoulder, I started thinking about Jesus carrying his tree up his hill. And right about then I understood that kind of pain.

Not the pain of the weight of the world, not the pain of the blood of the lamb, not that spirit pain. None of that.

What I felt was the pain of a man carrying lumber. Back breaking muscle grabbing deep down I'm gonna die carrying this goddam log pain.

Now that's the Jesus pain I understand. Carrying a piece of timber to where it's gotta go and neither of us knowing if we're gonna make it. It's enough to make you want to look up and shout out, Hey—You too busy to throw a little help my way?

The body's a strange piece of work. Just when I couldn't go no further—When my steps give out and I started sinking in the ground—my second wind came up from out of nowhere. And, something—set one foot in front of the other. And a little voice inside me said, You ain't finished yet.

Jesus must have got his second wind, too. And got his tree up his hill same as me to my burnpile. And now, here's the two of us, both facing the fire. Smiling through our sweat. 'Cause it don't matter now. We done what we had to do and what's done's done. And we could look each other right in the eye and say—damn, we did it. And if he was standing here right now, I'd sure as hell crack open a couple beers and sit him on my back porch with me. And I'd tell him all about what I was gonna do tomorrow. 'Cause my loggin' days sure as hell ain't done. And I'd say to him, How 'bout you, Mr. J, I bet you ain't done yet either? And I bet he'd just laugh and polish off that beer.

Nest Part I

When he crossed the threshold of the standing barn in the late morning, it was the smell that hit him first. A smell he'd recognized from a previous life. One that he'd packed up and walked away from, vowing never to return either by duty or memory. He'd buried nearly every sense from his desert days and did well over the last years creating a rough hewn blank spot in its place. Until this morning when the smell hit him, one that conjured up smoky visions from an old Aladdin's lamp on those ever-shifting sands.

The barn smell brought him back to the place where past and present merge: earthy, acrid, bittersweet. Frank scanned the seam where the splintered barnwood walls met the crumbling concrete floor. He was prepared to see something once living that had chosen the barn for its mausoleum, either by choice or by drawing the short straw. But he saw nothing. No sign of a tail or paw or parted fur. No stretched vellum skin over papier-mâché bones like the fox he'd seen along the road a few weeks earlier.

He took it in quickly. Eyes right, left, over each shoulder, then above, scanning the rafters. His training was still there, another thing that appeared when least expected. Above, he focused in on a circle of straw and mud, nestled into the join of a newer pine beam. A phoebe's nest.

Frank had seen Mr. and Mrs. earlier that spring, scouting out property, then zeroing in on a site inside the barn. Once they started, they were all business, taking turns bringing in material, laying out the foundation, erecting walls. It was clear that the couple had done this before and were well-schooled. And within a few days, they had finished. Then the real business began. Eggs were laid, warmth was generated and food was brought in. All for the bobbing heads that popped out and shrieked like tiny funhouse spooks.

Frank remembered getting dive-bombed when he'd gotten too close, but that was over a week ago. The funhouse mood had slipped away without notice. He stood in the middle of the cracking concrete slab awaiting some sound from the nest. A peep or chirp or chuck, whatever words the young phoebes spoke. But there was silence.

After a moment, he took the old paint-stained ladder that was leaning up against the barn's east wall and spread its rickety legs under the beam that held the nest. He slowly ascended the tilted steps until he was eye-level with the little ring of muddy straw and could peer inside.

Six heads, pointing upwards, mouths open, awaiting their next meal. Eyes gone and feathery down a dry, grey crust. Six frozen heads, stopped in time. And not an adult in sight. He'd seen a similar scene before. In that other life. In a house of desert bricks a world away. But now, it was here just a stone's throw from what he was calling home.

He descended to ground level and walked over to the pitted workbench to grab the oily workgloves, the ones he kept meaning to toss out, but like everything else in the barn and the outbuilding and the house had never moved from where Uncle Funtz had laid them. Frank climbed back up the ladder and lifted the nest off the beam. It took more effort than he had anticipated. The nest was now on its way to becoming part of the landscape like everything else within view.

He carried the nest with the six peepless birds into the woods to a clearing that he'd been working for several days.

Brush had been cut and the omnipresent stones, both large and small had been set aside in neat piles according to size for future use as drainage, pathways or garden borders.

He placed the nest with its contents on a patch of clean ground and then built, in diminishing sizes, a stone pyramid over it. Soon, the only trace was a triangle of rocks that had once been buried in the earth.

Nest Part II

The daylight filtered in slowly until the sun recognized that everything was in its place just as it had left it the day before. The heat would come later, one degree at a time. There was no need to rush and the end of day was not even a thought to be pondered. Frank stood in the back porch doorway taking in the morning. He held a mug of Oolong in his right hand, the cup of comfort, his wakeup call. His other hand held a slice of toast, buttered and unjammed. He'd stood there for a while, allowing the sun to take his surroundings from grey to color, from shadowy specter to full spectrum.

He liked watching the light or more precisely, what the light illuminated: an inventory of what was unseen in darkness now met his eye. His eyes scanned slowly to the barn door, or what was once barn door until it had fallen off, a week ago, leaving only a black hole that the sun had not yet found. His gaze drifted to the right, along the barn's paint-peeled "novelty-cut" siding to a golden, glowing ball, seemingly suspended in mid-air. He popped the last fragment of toast into his mouth, took a swallow of Oolong, and set out to see what the day had brought.

The golden ball changed into a soft-edged solid triangle, hip high, attached to the sturdy stalks of three yet to bloom Asiatic lilies. He closed in to see what could not be seen from the doorway. Slowly, it came into focus, blink by blink. A spider's nest of a hundred golden spiders, hatching in the morning light. Shimmering into being and vibrating with life. Working their way along their path of spun gold threads to waxy green leaves to begin the first day of what would be their lives.

Frank watched until he felt the sun's heat. A golden nest of golden spiders. Their gift to the sun and to themselves. Their silent music: a new melody from an old, familiar song.

Household
Gods

Crows chase the hawk at treetop.
Their spiral dance awakens me.
Will I be crow or hawk today?

Breaking ground like breaking bread.
Hands shape the brown dough.
A recipe as old as earth.

A new year brings the grass fed lamb.
Days are years.
Months, a lifetime.

The slug eats the primrose.
A dance inside the mirror.
The once upon has come.

The silk rose—flawless, fine and sure.
The cut rose bows and drops its petals.
Both vases stand empty.

The hawk carries the snake
out of view.
Neither will look me in the eye.

At the edge of a flat smooth stone.
A curled leaf or dead mouse?
Both and neither at this distance.

The woodpecker chips
the old apple tree.
Falling time is near.

The earth pushes treasures
to the surface.
A rusted razor and a worn boot heel.

The unseen songbird whistles
"Three Blind Mice".
The barn boards repeat the letter "Z".

Pheasants eat the seed I've sown.
Lines are drawn.
Lines are crossed.

In the old weathered barn,
housing the rusting and forgotten.
Remembering a father's words.

At dusk a dirty coin reveals itself
from under the raked mulch.
A good day's pay.

Ghosts surround us.
Their breath is heavy, warm and moist.
Their days no longer number.

The calico cat retires
from the Great Mouse Chase.
Cries of fear dissolve to laughter.

The turkey vulture swirls above.
Vital signs endure below.
Eyes are open.

Mounds of leaves.
A joyful end.
A long beginning.

Squirrel and rabbit, bird and me.
Footprints stitching snowquilts,
The Drunkard's Path Pattern.

Household
Tales
Part 3

Boneyard

The woods up the hill from the old farmhouse weren't dark or deep, but they did hold mysteries that slowly revealed with each visit. It was a place that readily brought a change of pace, as well as temperature for a post-lunch ramble after several hours of working in the sun.

Frank held two half-eaten chicken legs between the thumb and index finger of each hand, but they were starting to slip again. The generous coating of Cajun-Tang sauce had meandered in a dark brown rivulet down his forearms, and he'd already used up the seven paper napkins imprinted with the Roaring Bull BBQ's logo before he was even one step into the woods. It was a newly discovered slow food establishment that had become his mid-day takeout meatery after a morning of clearing prick berry, wild mustard, and fallen trees filled with woodpecker bulletholes.

Far up into one of the overgrowing paths, Frank was still gnawing at the last bits of chicken. It was better to be outside with his mess, he figured, than to get the last clean tea towel smudged, then left to fossilize in the broken, plastic tub in the pantry storeroom waiting for a laundry day that never seemed to fit into his schedule. Up past one of the outcropped boulders, Frank noticed that both chicken legs were about as clean as they could get. He couldn't see his face, but both of his hands were coated with BBQ sauce and he chuckled, thinking he must look like some highchair kid after a Gerber's dinner. He looked around for one of nature's napkins, and chose a low, leafy branch of an oak. He set down the two leg bones on a flat tabletop rock near ground level, then proceeded to clean himself up with the help of the branch. After wiping the salty sweet, addictive goo from his hands, arms and face, Frank slowly turned around full circle to see what would be a future project up in this quadrant.

Trees had fallen; Funtz's old pathways had grown over. There was a lot to be done, and Frank made a mental note that he hoped he'd remember: to visit this place again tomorrow and make a more definite commitment, and bring what needed to be done to this forgotten part of the world.

He'd heard all this before, over there, when he was part of a captive audience. He listened to middle-aged men and some women who'd make their clandestine swoops into the desert, surrounded by a moat of security and with enough bottled water so they'd never feel the chafe of dehydration. They wore dark suits but often had open shirt collars, both from the heat and to make them appear on the same team. They'd stand in front of Frank and his fellow grunts, and they'd talk about how they were all part of something big, a big picture, and how they were all making the world a better, safer place. And they would be thanked. And then the people in suits would leave. And life (and death) would go on the same as it had the day before they'd come.

Frank wanted it to be different here, to make a place that he could work with and not against. He was determined to come back to this spot tomorrow, and not just make another mental speech, but to do something with his own hands, to make what would always seem Funtz's place that he was caretaking, a place that he would approve of. Was it this spot where he'd fallen, like one of the old trees that he'd lived with for over half a century? Was this the place, by that boulder where he saw his land for the last time? Was that boulder Funtz's memorial stone that the land had marked to remember him? Was he, Frank, doing everything he could to continue the work that the Sellecks and all those after them had done to keep the land living? Or is it the land that brings life to those who work it? These thoughts brought Frank back out of the woods and to his back door. A faint smell of the BBQ sauce remained on his hands long into the evening even after two handwashings.

The next day, Frank didn't forget anything and that made him think that perhaps things were turning around. He did his morning chores, then headed off to the Roaring Bull BBQ for what was now his workman's takeout. After days of coming by, the folks at the BBQ knew him by face and order, if not by name. Another plus, Frank thought, a known entity coming to purchase a known commodity, his special. When he got back, he opened the styrofoam container, stuffed the nine paper napkins (they knew by now that he needed extras) into his jeans pocket, picked out two chicken legs smothered in sauce and headed out. He'd save the two thighs for supper, more of an evening meal than for lunch, and less transportable.

He'd gotten up to the spot in the woods he'd visited the day before, and was already finished with leg number one. As he started to create his mental to do list, he looked down at the table rock next to the big boulder. He remembered putting two chicken bones on that rock yesterday, but they were gone. Nothing was left, not a shard or a morsel of gristle. Something had carried them off or had enjoyed a late supper or early breakfast there at the table rock. There were certainly dogs in the area, but were there unleashed roamers who didn't eat out of a 40 pound bag? Wild dogs? The plural immediately surfaced. A pack of wild dogs. Or coyotes. Or had those Canadian wolves moved this far south. Fishercats. Or cats of any stripe or solid? That rumor of the Catskill Wildcat sailed through Frank's mind but escaped and ran off. But since he wasn't there to witness the feast, it could have been any or none of these. It could be something unknown to the general population, something spoken of in whispers and only in daylight and would cause both speaker and listener to cross themselves or at least spit three times over each shoulder. Frank knew he was traveling up a blind alley, and he wasn't going to camp out near the table rock to find an answer that might be disappointing. No, it was better not to know. That way, the bonetaker could be anything Frank wanted it to be and could change as often as the weather that rolled over the Gunks.

He finished the second chicken leg and placed both bones down on the table rock. An offering to whatever or whoever would come for it. Animal or animal-god. Or something greater than this. Something that watched over the seven acres from these stones; the place Funtz had known and whose secret he'd kept for all his years here. This place that Frank was brought to and the ritual that he had continued even without his knowing.

And so it began. Frank would keep the bones and fat and assorted scraps from his takeouts and his humble home cooking. And several times a week the offering would be made on the Table Rock. And the next time he went there all that he had left would be gone. A gift was given, and the house stood sound and safe.

The Hill

The rain had continued into its twenty-first day with the forecast calling for more. Water streamed down the hill, finding its way between rocks and over the feet of the oaks and sugar maples. It carried what little was left of hillside soil, bringing a muddy rivulet down to the stonewall and through its chinks where rounded edge met near square corner. The water continued onto one of the pathways that Frank had raked down to bare earth overlaid with wet newspapers then layered with leaf mold and wood chips to keep the weeds from sprouting for at least one season. But this was the path of least resistance and the stream found the easy way, both for today and for the future.

Frank decided to climb to the top of the ridge that a surveyor had marked with pink plastic ribbons, one on the east side and one on the west, the boundaries of Frank's land. The stream beyond the ridge ran the latitude of the property and often clogged with leaves and twigs and the occasional fallen limb. He'd even seen a fallen oak or maple cross the stream's path when its time was up, and would begin its new life settling back into the earth.

This growing gush of water, Frank reasoned, was surely due to the constant rains that would soon reach biblical proportions. Armed with his current favorite walking stick, a hardwood shillelagh with a German bent, he headed up the grassy rise to the connecting path that led up the hill. The wet leaves made for a slippery climb, but a slow and steady pace kept the course. He approached the top of the first crest and could see the swamp, once a fresh water pond with a wide array of aquatic and aviary life, he'd been told by one of the locals. But years of growth, collected sediment and human neglect had filled it in, leaving it a wetland to the ecologically educated and a swamp to the rest. Frank was firmly ensconced in the second group.

He was also both amused and bemused at being the owner of a swamp. He'd never owned a swamp, but now a swamp was added to his list of possessions. He was the keeper of topography, geography, geology and perhaps even archeology if he had the strength and knowledge to dig down far enough. An estate if he wanted to be pretentious. An estate of mind was more like it.

At the top of this first ridge, he stood midway between the eastern and western edges of the property. He also realized that he was halfway, or near enough, between his northern and southern boundaries. He jockeyed his position a few feet this way and that trying to imagine himself standing in the exact midpoint of his property. The middle of his world. The center of the universe with gentle rain refreshing his skin and breath.

Was this the place his Uncle Funtz had walked on that winter day? His last walk of his last winter? His last moment as caretaker of this postage stamp piece of earth before it passed on to Frank, without Frank ever knowing it was his? Was Frank standing in Funtz's footsteps on this mid-March day? Frank moved two steps to the right. Or was this the place? He could have danced all afternoon until he felt the right spot. He walked forward to the edge of the boulder where he could get a clear view of the house, the barn and ghost barn, the summer house, the last of the apple orchard and the stone walls that snaked along the boundary and nearly to the top of the hill. Yes, this might be it. Probably here where old Funtz sailed off to another new world. The undiscovered country from which he'd never return and would never want to.

"Hello."

"Hello." Frank replied without looking over his shoulder to where the greeting was coming from. He then turned to see three men in old work clothes and broad brimmed hats standing at the break of southeast stone wall that lead to an old logging road. The three stopped at the break to call to him, but kept the courtesy of not entering Frank's domain uninvited.

"Quite a spell of rain," the tall one said.

"Yes."

"I see your stream's swollen."

"Seems to be."

"We just cleared out mine. We're heading over to William's." The short one nodded to Frank. "We can give you some time. If you need."

Frank nodded. "I don't know this stream yet. Want to take a look?"

The mossy and tumbling-down rock wall, piled up waist high nearly two centuries ago, was the result of attempting to clear the land for farming, with varying success. A break in the wall, one of several along its not very straight path, had served as entrance and exit for people and livestock and small carts. The three men single-filed through and walked down one of the natural pathways between the trees and flattened rocks until they stood on the opposite side of the stream's swollen banks.

The tall man looked into the overflow. "I'm Haydock Carpenter. I'm up the hill and over that ways. This is Abraham Wooley, and Charles Young. They have farms down a ways to the west and east. Yes, I'd say you're pretty well clogged up."

"I'm Frank. Frank Closky." The men circled for handshakes.

"You're Funtz's boy?"

"He was my great-uncle, my father's uncle."

"Sorry he passed. A good man. You staying on?"

It was the first time that Frank had been asked this question. "A while, I guess."

Haydock smiled. "That's what I said. And it's been a while all right. This stream. It's like everything else around here. It takes time. But just keep watching. It'll tell you what you need to know. Probably spilling down to your back door."

Frank followed the water's path down the hill toward the house. "It's getting close."

Haydock was jovial, like a man who'd seen it all before, with an equal amount of concern. "Let's straighten this out. We're on our way to Charlie's to see his new calf. Came early." The other two men nodded to no one in particular and remained silent. The three companions were armed with odd hoes and long handled rake-like claws, similar to ones he'd seen in his barn, rusted but still useable. Abraham offered Frank one of these odd implements, again without a word, and Frank soon learned its subtleties after watching the three.

The men worked silently without stopping and without words. They cleared several years' worth of leaf and twig debris from the stream, freeing it to flow on its natural course along the ridge. It no longer eddied off into the downhill torrent that would turn Frank's house into lakefront property.

"I think you're squared away." Haydock flung his claw rake across his shoulder. The two other men followed suit.

Frank remembered his manners. "We're all pretty wet. We could head down and I could put on the kettle. Tea, coffee— it'll only take a minute."

Haydock shot a quick glance at the others, but they betrayed nothing through their face or body language. "Another time. Give us a rain check." And then the four laughed, the first sounds Frank had heard from Abraham and Charles. The laughter was short-lived, but it still sounded like the laugh among old friends. "We best be getting on. An oak bough broke though Charlie's coop and we better get that mended before his chickens float out to the Hudson. Besides, you'll want to check that runoff by your house. Let me know if there's anything more you need. I'm just down the road."

Frank ushered them to the break in the wall, then handed back the long-handled claw, two gestures that did not go unnoticed. "And let me know if *I* can do anything, whatever you need. I got a whole barn full of stuff." The men nodded. "Or just a cup of coffee or tea. Whatever." Frank left that door open in case his neighbors imbibed something stronger. He didn't know the local customs yet.

Abraham turned back to him. "Old Funtz used to make his elderberry blossom wine." That was the end of his conversation; he turned again and joined Haydock and Charles, heading south on the old logging road.

Frank looked at the stream now flowing freely, then at the three men, who nearly blended into the trees and brush and the darkening sky. Dusk had fallen quickly, making it hard to see anything in detail. He walked along the ridge to the jutting boulder that marked the trail and watched the last glow of the sun etching the western horizon of the hollow. He then looked down the hilly path and saw a second light and headed toward it.

It was not the light of eternity, or the light beckoning to the great unknown, or a beacon to steer his ship from dangerous, rocky shoals. It was so much simpler and so much greater. It was his kitchen light beside the sink on the automatic timer that he had set to turn on just in case. In case he was out and wanted to find his way back. The light that would lead him down the wet and rutted hill to the back door of the old house. Home now. To the place of beginning.

Laurence Carr, a writer of plays, fiction and poetry, has been published and produced throughout the U.S. and in Europe for over thirty years. His volume of micro-fiction, *The Wytheport Tales*, is published by Codhill Press, and he is the editor of *Riverine: An Anthology of Hudson Valley Writers* and the co-editor of *WaterWrites: A Hudson River Anthology*, also from Codhill. Over 20 of his plays and theatre pieces have been produced. His short play, *Porch by Moonlight* was named "Best of the Festival" at the Westside YMCA New Play Festival. His Off-Broadway play, *Kennedy at Colonus* received glowing reviews from the *NY Times* and was cited in the *Burns Mantle Best Plays Series*. Abroad, two plays were directed by Gregory Abels: *36 Exposures* in Prague and *Food for Bears* in Warsaw. His play for voices, *Baklava*, was commissioned by The Sound Foundation for National Public Radio, made into a short film, a stageplay and later broadcast over Slovak Public Radio in Bratislava. *Vaudeville*, published by Rising Moon Publishing, has had a dozen productions across the U.S. Along with Swedish colleague Malin Tybahl, he heads The Strindberg Project, creating new translations of the works of August Strindberg. He received a BFA from Ohio University and a Masters Degree from The Gallatin School of Individualized Study at NYU. He teaches Dramatic and Creative Writing at SUNY, New Paltz where he was awarded a "teacher of the year", directs the SUNY Playwrights' Project, and is a co-founder of The SUNY New Paltz New Play Festival. He's been a member of The Dramatists Guild since 1975.